The Sorceress of Song and Flame

Greylea Spell Series, Book 1

Siobhan Muir

ISBN-13: 978-1-947221-17-8

DEDICATION

Dedicated to my mother Kate, my aunt JES, and my late grandmother, Helen Mae. All these women encouraged me to write my fantasy stories, and here's one more. And yes, Gramma, I'm still including those "nasty bedroom scenes."

ACKNOWLEDGMENTS

Writing a book is never really a one-person job, and writing a set of companion tales is especially difficult. Keeping track of details is so much easier when you have help. Not only does it take a great deal of hard work, editing, and research on the part of the author to get things correct, but without my compatriots, there'd be a lot more mistakes.

Thanks to Cara Michaels for proposing the fun idea of Greylea to a group of us flash fiction writers. Great thanks to Nara Malone and Golden Czermak for making sure I wrote a good story without doing any disservice to autistic or Asian folks. Your help was invaluable. Huge thanks to Paige Prince for editing despite all sorts of medical challenges. And great thanks to Kris Norris for designing the cover with such challenging characters to depict. It was worth all the effort. You rock.

As always, great thanks to my readers for cheering me on. Y'all make my writing worth the detailed effort.

MAP OF GREYLEA

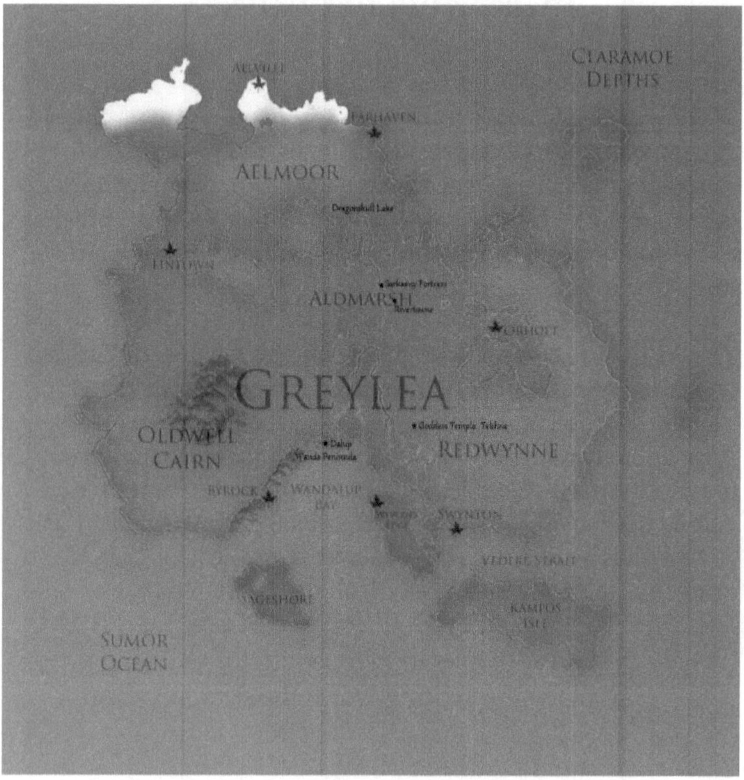

CHAPTER ONE

Matsuko

As an autistic person, confusion was normal for me. I'd been more sensitive to light, motion, and sound than neurotypical people since the moment I became aware, so I didn't always understand how other people took them all for granted. How did they ignore the brightness, the movement, or the constant noise?

Like what's going on right now.

Finding myself dressed in hooded robes on a dark, windy street I didn't recognize with blue fire filling my palms, I was understandably confused. And not in my usual way.

Last I checked, I'd been listening to some of my most favorite music, humming along as I ate my evening meal after work. Humming helped me release the pent-up emotions I'd experienced during the day and let them flow away. The scents of the briny coast and an approaching storm had filled my nose as the last rays of the sun caught the land before the clouds swallowed them. I'd tilted my head back and closed my eyes for just a moment.

The same moment the world tilted, and I threw my

hands out to grab the railing in front of me.

Except there was no railing, no sidewalk, no beach. And I'd set fire to a handcart and an unlucky pile of rags on either side of me.

The pile of rags jumped up, screaming, and ran down the cobblestone road between oddly ornate buildings no more than a single story tall. Surprise and panic ramped up in my chest and the flames from my hands grew larger.

Shouts came from the buildings around me, waking up what appeared to be a small seaside town. With burning lanterns instead of streetlights. And livery stables instead of covered parking. And swords instead of automatic rifles.

Unfortunately, that only ramped up my anxiety and I hummed louder, which made the flames leap a good two feet off my hands.

"Whoa!" I tried shaking them but that spread the fire in wider arcs. "Oh, glory, not good. Not good!"

When I stopped humming, the flames died back a bit. That made my scientific mind take note and I suddenly wanted to verify that sound increased the height of the flames. But the shouts of the armored men grew louder and more panicked, and some of them held what looked like crossbows.

Yeah, swords could be avoided for the most part. Crossbows were a sniper's weapon. I closed my eyes and silenced the music in my head. To my relief, the blue fire evaporated into the damp wind.

My relief was short-lived as the big men with the swords smelling of garlic and stale beer grabbed my arms and pinned them behind my back. I was so taken aback, I didn't make a move to escape. Panic started to rise again and with it, the fear that I'd set the men on fire. While I hated being manhandled, I didn't want to kill anyone if I could help it.

I tried to keep my mother's serenity sand garden in my head as they hustled me off the street and into an even more foul-smelling stone building. They said a few words to the intake officer who looked something like a BDSM Dom crossed with an executioner from the Spanish Inquisition. He even had a nipple ring on one beefy pec.

"What 'ave we 'ere then?"

"I reckon a sorceress or some such. Caught 'er settin' fire to the marketplace."

"This chit?" The intake officer stared down at me. "She don' look dangerous."

"She burned Crombe's market cart to a crisp."

"Why ain't she got the cuffs on, then?"

The guy holding me shrugged. "There weren't no resistance from 'er so we didn't worry too much."

The intake officer rolled his eyes at their unconcern. "That ain't the way to take in prisoners who done burnt shit down. Go on, then. Put 'er in the cell next to the thief. Maybe she'll make 'im sweat."

He chuckled darkly and they hustled me into a rabbit warren of dank cells. Sound echoed in the dark spaces like a dungeon out of an online video game and weird things looked at us from the cages. Some appeared vaguely humanoid, but others were decidedly not. *Was that a unicorn?* The horse-like creature was a mottled gray, had red eyes, and its horn twisted to a savage point. Definitely not the animals maidens were reputed to call.

They shoved me into an empty space with nothing but moldy straw, weeping stone walls, and a rusty bucket. I just managed to keep on my feet even as the guard pinched my ass and chortled before the gate slammed shut. Anger, fear, confusion swirled around my mind as I stopped in the center of the space, out of reach of anyone or anything near the walls.

"Sleep tight, girlie. Mayhap I'll be back later to try yer paces, yeah?"

Fear ignited to anger, literally, and one of my hands glowed. "Should we start right now?" I didn't dare throw it at him, but I wanted to see the fear reflected in his eyes. I couldn't control it, but he didn't know that.

He lost his smirk and skittered away from the cell with a muttered insult I ignored. I still needed to find some sort of anchor to reality, but none appeared to be forthcoming. The world around me had foul, alien scents and unfamiliar sounds, and I stood lost among them.

"You certainly have a way with the guards."

The smooth, cultured voice came from the cell to my left, and someone leaned forward into the limited light seeping through the bars from the smoky torches burning in the aisle.

I couldn't be sure he was speaking to me. I didn't know if he meant it as a compliment or in sarcasm. I still struggled with the basic niceties other people naturally understood.

"I wasn't going to let them do anything to me." I rubbed my arms with my hands, grateful I didn't set my own clothes on fire.

"Nor I. I may not be the greatest being out there, but I draw the line at taking a woman against her will."

I suppose that was comforting, though what he'd be able to do when iron bars separated us was unclear. I glanced around to find a place to sit, but the grime made me wrinkle my nose and avoid all surfaces. Who knew what crawled on the two stone walls? I shivered and wrapped my robes tighter around me.

Robes that aren't mine any more than the ability to control the fire in my hands.

Nothing made sense. I once heard people pinched themselves to wake up from dreams or nightmares or weird occurrences, but I'd never had to do that before. There were a lot of things I'd never done that had occurred in the last hour or so and that seemed to be the new normal.

So I pinched myself.

"Ow!" Other than pain, nothing had changed.

“What’s happened? Are you all right?” The figure relaxing in the other cell leaned forward and his eyes glowed like a cat’s for just a moment.

“I’m fine. Sort of, but not hurt. Much.” I frowned and met his hooded gaze. “Who are you?”

****

Arach

It was rare for me to find a human worth talking to, though the person in the cell beside me wasn’t completely human. She could be considered “other” or rather “more” than human. But she sat with a stillness not common in her species and that made her a rare treasure—at least to me. Humans had frenetic energy as if they had to experience everything within their meagre century of life. *Definitely an inefficient species.* My own people had millennia to learn and experience things.

“Who are you?” She faced me with her gaze landing in the vicinity of my chest. Most humans feared to look at a dragon square-on.

I rose to my full height and gave her sweeping bow. “Arach Uzekamanzi, part-time thief and full-time gentleman.”

She turned and bowed in return. “Matsuko Ishikawa. I’m an audiologist. Where am I?”

“You’re in the most illustrious prison in Wyvern’s Edge, the northernmost city on the Surland Peninsula of Greylea.”

“Where is that? Is it near Norway?”

I shook my head. “I don’t know Norway, but perhaps you’ve heard of Swynton? Byrock? Orholt? Farhaven?”

She shook her head. “No.”

I inhaled her scent, catching the fragrances of wizardly magic combined with divine grace.

By the ancient ones, she's gods-touched.

My interest in her trebled and my body reacted to such a potent combination of magic. She offered an intriguing puzzle to a time-weary dragon at loose ends—never a good combination—and treasure worth cultivating.

"It's reasonable to feel disoriented or lost. The wardens here aren't very forthcoming with information."

"I don't know what to feel." She reached up and tugged on her earlobes, closing her eyes. She took several deep breaths, making her ample chest rise and fall.

"Are you all right?"

"I don't actually know." She opened her eyes and glanced down at her hands, turning them in the dim light of the prison cell. "I don't know how I made flames come out of my hands."

"Perhaps a latent talent?"

She shook her head. "I don't have this talent." She tugged on her earlobes again. "My hands aren't burned. I could feel the heat, but it didn't hurt."

"Perhaps you've been blessed by the gods to wield such power."

She frowned as she raised her gaze. "I don't believe in god."

"That may change, m'dear." Lord Ignius knew I'd doubted his existence until he showed up and damn near singed my tail. I was a lot more careful about how often I threw my doubt around.

Matsuko frowned and shook her head. "None of this makes sense."

I leaned against my cell door. "What would make sense to you?"

"Starbucks and my cellphone full of music. Yoga pants and a Toyota Prius. Maybe a good Marvel movie. Do you think Steve Rogers got together with Peggy Carter in the new timeline?"

I frowned. None of the things she said made sense to

me, but she sounded wistful, like these were common things in her life. "Uh…"

"Oh, I know, no spoilers, it would ruin it. But do you think that's less fantastical than being able to shoot fire from my hands? I mean, no matter what, I do have a good memory and I remember shooting fire from my hands, and that makes less sense than movie magic."

She suddenly pressed herself against the bars between our cells. "Tell me the truth. Where am I really? Did Universal Studios put together a Lord of the Rings action set and we're in it?"

I laughed. "My lady, the universe often puts events in our path so we may learn, but this Lord of the Rings doesn't exist. Now there is a Lord of Stones, but he's a rather dreary old mage who keeps shiny rocks and says they're full of power. Fool."

Matsuko frowned and despite her fearsome visage, I remained charmed. "You have no idea what I'm talking about, do you?"

"Not a bloomin' clue."

She sighed and turned her back against the bars, sliding down into the moldy straw. "I have to get out of here and get home. I don't belong here."

I chortled. "Oh, my dear, none of use *belong* here. We're just here temporarily."

She glanced at her hands and tilted her head. "I'd rather not be here at all. I almost blew up the town. If I knew how to control…whatever this is, I could blow the door open. But I don't have the skill."

I perked up at her statement. "Perhaps I can help teach you to hone your skills. But this isn't the most convenient place to do so. I propose we leave."

She snorted with what sounded like amusement. "Absolutely. Leaving would be lovely. Do you happen to have the keys to this establishment?"

Her sarcasm delighted me. "No, but I know where they

can be found, and the guards tend to talk. They don't think I hear them, but I do. Exceptional hearing, you see. But we don't actually need the keys. Just a plan to get past them once the doors are open."

"Wait, you can get out of here anytime you want?" She tilted her head with a frown. "Then why are you still in here?"

I laughed as I stretched. "I needed the break. My father and my enemies can't get to me here. I was using it as a safe place to rest with both eyes closed. But now, I'm rested and adventure awaits."

I strode to the door and inserted a claw, rattling the tumblers of the old lock. They turned surprisingly easily considering how grimy they were, and the door squeaked open.

"Ready to leave, my dear?"

She gaped at me as I stepped into the main aisle.

CHAPTER TWO

Matsuko

Arach unlocked the cell door and stepped out into the aisle.

He's here because he needs a nap?

I gaped at him as he moved to my door and with a flick of his wrist, unlocked that, too.

"Are you coming?"

I scrambled to my feet, but still hesitated on the threshold. Could I just walk out? I'd torched some of the buildings and though it had been an accident, I'd still done it. But I didn't know the rules and I didn't want to see what they'd do to an Asian woman they felt was a threat.

Shooting looks either way down the aisle, I stepped out beside the man who'd become my impromptu friend.

"Excellent. Let's be on our way. Hopefully, the guards will be gaming as is their wont and we'll slip out without them seeing us."

He gestured ahead and I followed him down the grimy hallway toward the front of the jail. The other prisoners watched us, though none of the made a move toward the aisle except the mean-looking unicorn. It tilted its head as I passed, like it considered me an intriguing snack, and I hurried my steps away.

Voices from the guards filtered to us from their wardroom and the scents of unwashed male bodies increased. Not that the jail smelled wonderful to begin with, but unwashed men plus the heat of a smoky fire made for a pungent combination. I swallowed hard against the stench as fear tried to crawl up my throat.

Quiet as a mouse, Matsuko.

I used to be very good at making myself small and quiet. But I'd grown and could shoot fire from my hands. That was distinctly not quiet.

Arach paused just before the light spilling into the hallway from the wardroom and placed a finger to his lips. I understood his suggestion and nodded as he moved to the wall farthest from the doorway to peer into the guards' space. I don't know what he saw, but he nodded to me and darted through the light to the other side without a sound. Then he motioned to me to copy his moves.

I bit my lip and shifted to the opposite wall, anxiousness ramping up in my chest. Would the guards see me? Would they turn and look just at the wrong time? My hands started to tingle and I glanced down. Blue sparks flickered over my fingers, and I clenched them into fists as I shot a helpless look at Arach. Nothing like setting off fireworks when going for stealth.

He grimaced and looked around like he was trying to figure out what to do. I tried to picture the serenity garden to calm myself down again.

They don't know you're here. They can't see you. They can't hear you. Calm down.

I took a deep breath and focused on letting the fearful energy slide away from me. Thankfully, it took the sparks with it and my hands stopped tingling. I blew my breath out and looked for Arach. He nodded and motioned me to come to him on the other side of the light. I gritted my teeth and pulled up my hood before I straightened my shoulders and skittered across the open space.

Please don't see me. Please don't see me. I'm nothing but a flickering shadow in the firelight.

It seemed like as good a mantra as any, and miraculously, it worked. No one looked up at the wrong moment or sounded the alarm. We'd made it beyond the wardroom. But we still had to get past the BDSM Dom intake officer at the front of the jail. While he hadn't been concerned with me, I didn't want to test my random powers against him.

Again, Arach took the lead and peered around the edge of the counter near the door. I couldn't see much, but he motioned to crouch down beside him.

"The hooded fool is nodding in his sleep. Not sure why he hasn't found his bed yet, but he's not awake. Stay crouched and I'll get the door open, then you can slip out silently and we'll be home free."

"Okay. I understand. Do you think the door will be quiet enough?"

He grinned in the limited light. "We'll find out, won't we?"

When I gaped at his craziness, he added, "It's all part of the challenge."

I shook my head as he crawled away. *Sweet glory, he's totally insane.*

He got the door open without a sound and I crawled to him without the intake officer noticing we'd gone. We even got outside the jail without mishap. And then everything fell apart.

Apparently, the reason the intake officer hadn't found his bed yet was he waited for the arrival of new guards fresh out of training from General Warmonger, an ironic name that made me roll my eyes.

The men he expected arrived just as we got out the door.

“Oy! Who are you lot and what do y’think yer doin’?”

After the silence of our escape, the head guard’s loud voice surprised me and released my delicate hold on my emotional state. My hands tingled with heat and power, and blue fire rose like burning swords from each palm.

Guards surged out of the armored coach and surrounded us.

“Think that’s the sorceress Twilly was talkin’ about, Captain?”

“Yeah, I’d say that’s her. Are you lot gonna just stand there or cuff her?”

I shot a look at Arach, but he’d disappeared and left me to face the guards alone.

So much for an adventuring friend.

I didn’t know the rules in the village, but I knew enough to want to get away from the sneering guards and the jail. How, I hadn’t figured out, but if I needed to use my flaming hands, I would.

I hummed a little tune, something from a Celtic singer in my world, and the fire swords shortened but intensified. I wanted to tell them to back off, to leave me alone or I’d offer them a display of fireworks, but the humming helped me focus and I couldn’t spare the breath.

“Bloody gits, get her!”

That was all the initiation I needed. I focused the sound and the power on the armored wagon. If they were going to threaten me, I’d remind them why they threw me in jail in the first place.

“Aleuces, aleuces, ale-ooh-ooh-ooh goodbye.”

I threw the flames at the wagon like softballs, each splattering against the wooden sides like paint balls. Unlike paint, the flames suck to the wood and licked upwards in a deadly dance. They were beautiful and I wanted to watch them consume the wagon as the men ran around in panicked circles.

“By all that’s holy, run, Matsuko!”

Arach's shout shocked me into moving and I bolted away from the burning vehicle as I looked for my erstwhile jail mate. I was reasonably sure there hadn't been any people inside the wagon. The idea that someone might have been trapped inside when the explosion of blue flames engulfed it sickened me. I damn near vomited as I tried to run, tears blinding my eyes.

Gotta get away. Gotta get away.

The problem was I didn't know where I would go. Heck, I didn't even know if going was the best path. I wasn't a nature-lover by any stretch of the imagination. Safety had always been found inside where there was running water and heat.

I headed out of town toward a forest swathed in misty fog with nothing but the road beneath my feet to indicate my path. The air smelled wet and dank, like the laundry room in my apartment building back home, and I shivered with distaste.

Glory, will I ever be warm and dry again?

I hated winter in western Washington for that reason. It seemed to go on forever and I feared I'd never be warm again.

I entered the trees and an eerie silence enveloped me. I stopped and froze, the only sound my harsh breathing. I spun, looking back the way I'd come, but I only found more road, more mist, and more trees.

Good glory, it's like the road from Lord of the Rings and the Nazgul rider.

I half-expected some huge, cloaked guy to come riding up on a horse bleeding from nasty festering wounds. I tried to listen for pursuers, but my heartbeat had grown so loud, it took all my attention.

Where was Arach? For that matter, where was I?

I gotta get off this road.

If movie magic had taught me anything, no one should be in the middle of a road cutting through a misty forest.

Too many things would find and hurt me.

Voices and a silhouette sent me back into motion perpendicular to the road's path and I leapt down the berm into the leaf detritus. I ducked down and tried to make myself as small as possible. Hopeful the mist would hide me well enough to let me escape their notice.

I hid my face in my arms and held my breath. *Please don't find me. Please don't see me.*

The clothing I wore had been dark—I hadn't looked at it too closely—and I hoped it would help keep me concealed.

Seconds passed and my heart thundered, but I kept my face pressed into my arms. Eventually, when nothing happened, my panic receded, and I was able to lift my head. The air had grown warmer and the mist had thickened. I could see less than I had before. Sound seemed muted and the light grew dim.

I swallowed hard and strained to see the road above my hiding place. Swirls of fog showed movement, but I couldn't tell what was there. I bit my lip and wrapped my arms around myself as I watched for danger, hoping I'd been forgotten by whomever chased me.

"She can't have gone far. Keep searching the woods, but don't kill her. The general says we must bring her back alive. Roughin' up ain't a problem, but definitely alive."

That answered if they were after me or not. I tried to decide if hiding was the best course when a whistle grew louder in the air. It reminded me of the sounds of the World War Two bombs as they dropped on ground targets, and I shot to my feet. A look at the sky showed nothing but mist.

"What in the gods' names is that?"

"Holy fuck! DRAGON!"

Crimson fire bloomed on the road, lighting up the world and throwing shadows among the trees. Men in armor went up like tinder and the screams competed with the roar of the flames.

Sweet glory.

I watched in horror as they burned, unable to run or heck, even scream. I stood, stupefied at the carnage. Which was why I didn't see the dragon come back for me and did nothing but shriek when its talons closed around me. It yanked me off my feet and carried me into the misty sky.

I clutched the huge hand wrapped around me and held perfectly still. Struggling meant I'd be free—free to fall to my death as we soared over the misty woods below. How the big beastie could see where it was going, I had no idea. There was no rhyme or reason to its path, and I was only along for the ride.

I tried to get a good look at the dragon, but it clutched me to its warm scaly breast in one gold, tan, brown, and russet-scaled hand. Despite the wind rushing past my face, I could damn near hear the thumping of its heart against my back.

Or maybe that's my heart.

I gulped and watched the misty forest slide beneath us. I had the weird sense of déjà vu, like I'd seen this in a movie, maybe the one with the blue humanoids with long tails. But eventually the forest thinned, and we rose above the clouds into sparkling sunshine.

There was something terribly exhilarating about sailing over the world in an open-canopy airship. Okay, a dragon wasn't an airship and the only reason I was exposed to the elements was because it had me in its claws, but the experience of seeing the world from high up was literally awesome.

Eventually, the ground beneath us became rolling grassy hills and my ride dropped altitude as a lake and some random buildings came into view. The dragon set us down beside the small glacial lake with the dexterity of a hummingbird.

As soon as the beastie let me go, I scrambled away from it, hoping to get out of reach. But the creature rumbled what sounded like a chuckle and reined me in with its tail and one talon.

Penned like the ducks and geese in that old children's song.

I could just imagine the dragon saying, "you're gonna grease my chin before I leave this town-o."

I'm so screwed. Yeah, I'd be nothing more than a red smear. *At least I'm not a crispy critter like the guards.*

I backed away from its head but stopped. Where the hell could I go? It wasn't like it couldn't reach me. Hell, all it had to do was sneeze and I'd be done like an overcooked steak. I swallowed hard and wrapped my arms around my middle, hoping the end would be quick.

But the earth-toned dragon heaved what sounded like an exasperated sigh and closed its eyes. I thought it might be going to sleep, but instead it started to shimmer and fade, like something out of a sci-fi cartoon. The air shifted, pulling me forward a few steps, and I flung my arms out to steady myself before there was a subtle *pop!* And the dragon disappeared.

In its place stood my erstwhile partner and fellow escapee, Arach Uzekamanzi.

I blinked. "What the hell?"

"I'm not the one you expected?"

"Am I crazy? There was A DRAGON RIGHT THERE!" I didn't normally shout, but it had been a rough…day? Morning? Few hours? "Where's the dragon? How did you get here? What the hell is going on?"

For just a moment, he wore an expression of confusion.

Yeah, like I'm the one who's being weird.

But then his eyes widened and his jaw dropped. "You've never seen Dragonkin before?"

"Is that some sort of trick question? Dragons are *mythical beasts*. They don't exist."

He threw his head back and laughed. "Oh, my dear, you're a treasure. Dragons *do* exist, and I am one, though my father may contest it."

I rubbed my eyes. "No, no, no. First, my hands throw fire—"

"An aspect that is very sexy, I might add."

"And now the guy who breaks me out of prison is…is…"

"Dragonkin," he supplied helpfully.

"The world is going to hell in a handbasket."

Arach smirked. "I didn't know hell could fit in a handbasket. Does the type of weave matter?"

"Shut up or I'll throw fire at you." I rolled my eyes.

His smirk bloomed into a grin. "Promise?"

"Oh, sweet glory, you're insane!" I yelled again but I couldn't seem to keep my frustration in check. "I told you before, none of this makes sense." I closed my eyes and fisted my hands, trying to remember the patterns that helped me when I got into a loop.

I started humming my favorite rock ballad and the strains of music wrapped around me like a warm cloak. I kept my eyes closed and let the sounds roll through the emotional loop threatening to derail me. In my mind, I could hear the drums, electric guitars, and keyboards ramping up into a powerful thumping beat in my breastbone. I let my body move to the music, falling into the energy building within my mind.

It was like I'd arrived at a concert in full swing and when I opened my eyes, I could hear the sounds around me. But that wasn't what surprised me.

Arach stared at me with what looked like awe. "Sweet gods. Marry me."

"You're unbelievable." All the sounds vanished and so did the blue flames flickering around me. "I can't marry you. You're not even human."

"Neither are you, my dear." He caught one of my hands and the anxious energy pounding in my head settled into a contented hum just behind my breastbone. "You're something other than I've never encountered before. A true treasure and oddity. I collect such treasures."

All that would've sounded romantic until his last sentence. I yanked my hand from his.

"I'm not a collector's piece, a freak of nature, or an oddity to be displayed. If that's all you see me as, you can fly your dragon ass somewhere else."

I turned and walked away from him. I had no idea where I was going. I didn't know the way home or if "home" even existed anymore. But I wouldn't stay there and listen to him compare me to a lovely crystal or stone he'd found on the beach one day. I'd often been compared to a cute doll or a crane with my height and lankiness. I was the tallest person in my family and the only autistic person. I'd never been ordinary, and it looked like that trend would continue.

CHAPTER THREE

Matsuko

"Matsuko, wait." He caught up, but to his credit, didn't touch as he skidded to a stop in front of me. "Wait. I'm sorry. It was meant to be a compliment. But I see you didn't take it as one. Forgive me."

I didn't often cry. Emotions were overwhelming and didn't adequately express what I needed, so I usually pushed them to the back of my mind. But too much of my past had been defending myself—to teachers, to strangers, to employers, and finally to clients. Some had been thrilled with my ability to recognize the patterns that would help them heal faster. Others found my skills to be a sideshow attraction like a performing dog or a dancing bear. Very few saw me as a person who viewed the world through a filter very different from their own.

Yeah, an oddity and a treasure to be collected like Arach said.

"It's not a compliment when you don't see me as anything other than a collectible. I'm not a doll or a trophy. I'm a person!"

The tears burst out and slid down my face before I

could stop them. I'd learned that tears made people uncomfortable along with the crying and screaming, so I tried to keep them to a minimum. But once they'd started, it was very hard to stop, and the only solution I'd found was humming. Which, in this world, set off my newfound magic.

Flames leapt around me with frightening intensity, making me hum louder, which made the flames grow. The escalating circle of emotions spiraled beyond my control and I'm sure I looked like that comic book character who turned into a living flame.

To my surprise, Arach grasped my shoulders and turned me to face him.

"Matsuko, you are a person, a far more interesting one than I've met in a long time. You're valuable to me because you're one of the few who will look at me and talk to me without fear."

I stared at him, watching the flames dance around his body like a living cloak, but they didn't burn him at all. In fact, they made him beautiful. His eyes were the same color as the amber encasing an ancient flower I had on my desk at home, but they glowed with the ethereal light of my blue flames. The light flashed in his shoulder-length dark brown hair and appeared like a crown over his head.

I'm not the oddity. He is.

His touch calmed my unruly emotions and allowed me to settle, reducing my tears and the flames.

"I don't understand."

He gave me a rueful half smile. "You really aren't from this world, are you?"

I shook my head, though the answer seemed obvious.

"Come sit with me for a bit. I liberated some provisions from the village and brought them with us. Are you hungry? My governess often told my brothers and me nothing could be solved on an empty stomach."

He drew me over to a downed tree and dabbed my tears

with the edges of his shirt sleeves.

"Better?"

I nodded because it was what he wanted to hear, but nothing felt better. He lifted a knapsack with leather ties and opened it to show me its contents.

"They provided ale, cheese, some savory sausage, and bread. Not the most elegant of meals, but certainly able to take the edge off."

He handed me the flagon of wine and I grimaced. I didn't like alcohol. It made me feel even more out of control than I usually was with my difficulty interpreting social cues.

"Is there water?" I picked up the bread and tore a chunk off.

He gasped and his eyes widened. "You don't drink ale?"

I debated answering him with the whys behind it but decided it wasn't worth the effort. "No."

He waited to see if I'd elaborate, but I kept eating and he eventually sniffed the contents of the flagon before he grimaced and poured it out. "Probably the best choice, considering."

"Considering what?"

"That it smells like pig's swill." He shook his head and rose. "I'll find some water."

I watched him go and wondered for the tenth time where I truly was and how I'd gotten there. I didn't believe in dragons or magic, but I found myself in a place with both. I no longer questioned that. But there didn't seem to be an explanation as to *how* I'd gotten there.

I hadn't attended any parties or events where drugs or hallucinogens had been offered. I'd been eating dinner. At home. Alone. I'd prepared the meal myself from fresh ingredients and no one had altered the food before I'd consumed it.

So, I'm not drugged or in a drug-induced fantasy.

And I'd pinched myself while in the jail and felt pain, but hadn't woken up, which meant I was awake as I already suspected.

"So like it or not, understand it or not, I'm here where magic and dragons exist."

"And I, for one, am grateful." Arach returned with a full flagon of water.

"Why?" I took the flagon and drank, pleased with the temperature of the water.

"You don't prevaricate, do you?"

"No. Why are you grateful I'm here?" I set the water down and kept eating.

"Because you are interesting and unique, and unlike anyone I've met before."

"I know. An oddity." The old anger and frustration rose again, and defeat thumped in my chest. I hadn't been valued beyond an interesting conundrum in my world, either.

He shook his head. "I should've chosen my words more carefully. I can see you don't use euphemisms."

"They only waste time and confuse people. It's better to be direct."

"Clearly, you've never lived in a royal court."

It was an odd thing to say, but I shook my head. "No, I haven't."

"That's another thing that I like very much about you." He settled beside me and selected some sausage with the bread. "From now on, I promise to be very plain with you so there are no more misunderstandings between us. I find you unique and valuable because you don't play word games or say anything you don't mean. And if you don't understand something, you ask. These are unusual traits among people, humans included. And you don't fear talking to me, which is unusual."

"Why? Are you unkind when speaking to people?"

He laughed. "Not unless it's necessary. People fear

talking to me because I'm a dragon, and technically, I'm a prince."

"You're a prince? As in royalty?"

He nodded, a half-smile curling his lips. "Yes, prince number three of four, and child number six of ten."

"Wow, big family." I didn't say more because that was all there was to say.

"That's it? Just 'big family'?"

I blinked. "Yes. Is there anything else to say?"

"You're not surprised I'm the Third Born Prince of Dragonkin?"

I tilted my head and frowned. "Do I need to be? Will there be a quiz later or some sort of protocol I'll have to follow because of that?"

He laughed. "There might be. But you really don't care about my heritage, do you?"

I stopped myself before I spoke without thought. "Is it important to you?"

"What, my heritage?" When I nodded, he shook his head. "It only matters when I need to deal with my father or brothers. Otherwise, no, it doesn't matter to me. It never helped when I needed it."

Some emotion colored his words, but I couldn't decipher it. He didn't sound happy, though, so I filed it away with Disappointment and Frustration.

"Then I will value it as part of your past and remember it if we ever have to visit your family, but it won't be the most important thing about you."

He tilted his head. "What *is* the most important thing about me from your perspective?"

I shrugged. "Right now, it's that you are a dragon and know more about this world than I do. I don't even know why or how I got here."

He laughed. "Not what I expected you to say, but I like the way you think. And I think I know someone who could help you figure out why you're here."

I sat up straighter and chewed on the food. "Who can do that?"

He extended his arm and pointed toward an unusual building higher up on the hills above us. "Do you see that place up there?"

It looked a little like a bunch of hoodoos, the rock formations left by mechanical weathering processes from rain and wind.

I nodded. "What's in it?"

"For me, knowledge, understanding, and occasionally, peace." He shrugged. "For others, who knows? But for you? I would guess it'll provide answers. It's the temple for the goddess Tekhne, goddess of arts, crafts, and music."

My first thought was to deny the existence of a goddess, but after seeing Arach shift from being a dragon, I'd had to revise my assessment of the world.

"Why do you think she'd have answers for me?" I drank more water.

He shrugged. "You hum when you're nervous and your magic seems to respond to music. Given her specialty, I figure she'll know the most about you, and if not, she'll know who you can ask."

I capped the water flagon and stared at the temple. "Do gods really talk to you here?"

"Only when you ask nicely."

I waited for him to laugh, but when he didn't, I revised my world view again. *Dragons exist. Gods exist, and you have to ask nicely.* I'd learned early on that whatever rules the people around me felt were true, was the way things were done, even if I saw something different. It was less distressing to just agree to what they said than to point out the inconsistencies of their reasoning. I'd learned to modify my programming, using the if-then algorithm to help me navigate the inconsistencies.

We finished our meal as I kept going over what I'd learned. The repetition of my memories and events helped keep me calm and in control of the flaming magic I had literally at my fingertips. Arach packed everything back into the satchel he'd liberated and held his hand out to me.

"Shall we visit the temple?"

I glanced at his hand as I stood. "The temple is that way." I pointed over his left shoulder.

He laughed. "Yes, I was offering you a hand up."

"Why?"

"It's the gentlemanly thing to do." He shrugged.

"Are you a gentleman?" I fell in beside him as we started the climb up the hill.

"Most of the time."

He said nothing else as we climbed, and I didn't have a rejoinder. Besides, the hill was steep enough to require the path we found to switchback on itself at least six times. I kept my thoughts focused on the new algorithm I'd discovered and the breath sawing in and out of my chest as we made our ascent. Arach didn't seem to be winded at all.

Of course not. He probably has the strength of a dragon, too.

When we reached the crest of the hill, it flattened out as if someone had cut the top off to ensure the maximum level space to build a building. From a distance, it had looked like natural rock formations, but up close I could see the deliberate design to make it appear natural. Each of the five towers appeared like twisted wind sculpted stone strata that sparkled with mica. The colors ranged from deep black at the base and ended with almost white at the tips. It took me a moment to recognize the sequence of mafic to silicic geologic pattern that my father had studied in college.

There were seven alcoves on the front but only one was a set of double doors. The alcoves flanking the door held statues, but the alcoves on the outside of the statues held windows. After looking at the towers, alcoves, and windows, I recognized a pattern. All the spaces and objects were made up of prime integers. Five towers, seven alcoves, three openings, two windows, two doors, and when we stepped into the interior, the temple held a pentagon shape with thirteen columns to uphold the roof. There were eleven prayer stations, two per wall and one in the center, where supplicants could bring their offerings.

Two more windows looked out on the green rolling hills on the back walls and a single skylight shone down on the central prayer station. Someone had been by recently, because an old lute and some purple flowered plants that looked like lavender were left in the glowing light around the feet of wide cushioned bench. The walls glittered with more of the mica I'd seen outside, and the floor held tiled mosaics in green and blue.

Energy rippled through the air as I stepped over the threshold and a sense of recognition hit me, like the place knew me though I'd never seen it before, not even in dreams.

Dreams are messages from our family guardians, from their divine connection. My grandmother's voice echoed in the back of my head. She'd been convinced that the visions we saw in sleep were hints of what was to come, rather than our subconscious reporting the events we'd already seen.

I glanced back to see where Arach had gotten to and found him kneeling with his head bent in respect. I blinked, having never seen him so reverent, and turned back to look at the bench. Where it had once been empty, a being sat cross-legged with an Indian guitar-like instrument I'd heard called a vina on their lap. Metallic lace-like leggings traced up the calves and thighs, and a matching set covered the arms, all four of them, to the wrists. Tattoos etched the sides of the torso and wrapped across the breasts on the chest, disguising the bare nipples in ink. While the body stature appeared feminine, I couldn't be sure which pronoun would encompass the person.

Glowing white eyes opened and looked at me, the head

tilting to one side as a long braid of black hair slid over one shoulder.

"Welcome, Matsuko Ishikawa."

CHAPTER FOUR

Matsuko

While I'd been welcomed plenty of places, it was unnerving to have a being I'd never seen before greet me by name.

"Hello." I nodded, aware that I might have been missing the proper protocols in greeting, but not sure what else would be required of me.

The lips quirked into a smile as one pair of hands plucked the vina. Another hand pointed over my shoulder.

"Rise, Arach Uzekamanzi, Third Born Prince of the Dragonkin, part time thief, merc-for-hire, and warrior only if necessary."

I hadn't heard the other descriptors, but somehow, they didn't surprise me. Arach struck me as a person who'd do some things just for kicks while avoiding others.

"Honorable Tekhne, I'm grateful to be welcome into your temple again." He rose, but instead of his usual cocksure strutting, he'd taken on a demeanor of reverence.

"I'm sure you're happy to be somewhere your enemies wouldn't expect to find you." Tekhne's voice was dry, and an amused smile curled the goddess's lips as they fixed their gaze on me. "But I'm glad you brought me the Sorceress Matsuko Ishikawa. I've been waiting for you."

"You were expecting me?" Unease slithered through my gut. I'd never found it to be good when someone I didn't know knew about me.

"Oh yes. When our call went out for champions, I didn't know what to expect, but I was very aware of when you arrived."

You mean when I nearly burned down a town? But my mind caught up on the rest of their words.

"You put out a call for champions? What kind of champions? To do what?" I probably should have waited for the goddess to answer my questions, but my nervousness had ramped up again.

"Be at peace, Matsuko." The goddess rose from the bench and gauzy fabric swirled around their body as their eyes blazed. "I shall relate to you the tale behind your arrival and why you and your companion have been chosen for this quest."

Music rose, setting us up for an audio story time. It swelled in the temple and the walls disappeared until a vast sky of stars spread out behind Tekhne.

"In the time before time, when the world was new and all the peoples were becoming, we gods found our place and eminence. We were given temples and sacred spaces where all could come to worship. And we found balance in our respective tasks, guiding and teaching the peoples about the wonders of the world."

"Oooh, this is gonna be good." Arach wove his fingers together and licked his lips like a kid waiting for a treat.

"Shh."

"But a few scant centuries ago, as humans measure time, one of our number, Anima the Soul Keeper, began to show signs of disturbance."

The space image shifted until we were given a vision of a feminine-looking being with emerald-green hair and matching eyes, bright red lips, and olive skin. The gaze of the being seemed to stare straight through me into my very Self and I shivered with awareness.

"Anima stopped young souls from being born and yet let others live well beyond their time, warping and harming the people she was meant to guide. The council of the gods made the decision that she must be protected against those who would seek to use her power over death for their own ends. So we placed her in a protective space and lulled her into rest while we tried to learn how to heal her."

"So you stuck her in a prison and drugged her." I hadn't meant my voice to come out quite so flat, but there had been a time my parents hadn't known what to do with me. They'd taken me to an institution and left me there so the doctors could figure out what was "wrong" with me. Only my grandmother had protested, and she eventually rescued and raised me herself.

Tekhne had the grace to grimace. "We didn't know what had befallen Anima and we didn't want her harmed while we learned what needed to be done. But the peoples of our world are very curious, often dangerously so, and one such group of would-be adventurers broke into Anima's sacred—"

"Prison."

"—chamber and stole the artifacts that kept her dreaming in serenity. One such artifact is Tekhne's Song." Tekhne waved a hand and a large blue gem that looked like a star sapphire appeared. "This Song Stone holds my divine voice and whoever controls the stone may use that voice at their discretion."

I narrowed my eyes as I tried to figure out what they weren't saying. "You mean, if someone good got a'hold of the Song Stone, they could use it to convince people to be more loving or generous. But if someone bad got a'hold of it, they could use it to…what, coerce folks to start wars, steal property, kill people?"

"Exactly."

Oh. "And who has the stone now?"

Tekhne's expression grew cold and forbidding as they waved their hand and the scene changed. A white man with pale blonde hair, icy gray eyes, decked out in more armor than I'd seen on a SpecOps soldier in the movies, sat on a gray destrier in matching plate armor and surveyed something I couldn't see. There was a cruelty to his expression that made me shiver.

"We believe General Dorian Warmonger has the Song Stone."

"Wait, wait, stop. Dorian 'Warmonger'? Are you serious right now? This guy has a name like that and you didn't see him coming? Warmonger, literally a 'dealer or trader in war.' No one thought that might give a hint to what he's up to?" I raised an eyebrow.

"I believe he's only recently taken up that moniker." Tekhne smirked a bit as they shifted the view in the temple. "But he does embody the name exceedingly well."

I snorted. "Yeah. He does that. If he'd chosen "butterflyslayer" or "Knittingmaster" no one would've taken him nearly as seriously."

To my surprise, the goddess laughed. "That is certainly true. And no one would write songs about the Knittingmaster."

"Not unless they'd gotten into some good Smokegrass, but going down that road is a bad trip, believe you me." Arach shook his head ruefully and I filed that away to ask about later.

"So what does this have to do with me?" The narrative they'd told me was wonderful but I wasn't even supposed to be there, much less had a hand in losing the stone in the first place.

The view changed again, filling with a group of hooded figures all swaying around a central firepit.

Now there's a white man's fire for sure.

In the vision, the hooded figures waved their hands and swayed and waved some more as the fire grew brighter and larger. Rainbow lights flashed in streaks around the flames until they rose in a multicolored ball of light above a curiously colorless fire. The ball swirled with the chakra colors, sparking with flashes of white and silver as it spun above their heads.

"The human magic community determined they needed heroes to help right the wrongs of the past, and to bring back the stolen artifacts. They constructed a summoning spell of great magnitude that encompassed all the elements of the gods and world."

Tekhne waved one of their hands. The brilliantly-colored ball in the vision exploded in a flash of white light and a percussive wave knocked all the figures down and spread beyond view. It even blew the fire out until the figures sat in the darkness. Tekhne waved away the images.

"This spell was meant to summon heroes from the farthest reaches of our lands, but something went wrong."

"Obviously." I snorted.

Tekhne scowled. "Instead of bringing heroes from our world, it brought them from another world and dropped them here. And not just the souls. Apparently, without Anima's direction, whole people are being transported here."

I blinked. "Wait a minute. If I was brought here from my world to yours, how do I suddenly have the ability to set fire to my hands? And not just any fire, but *blue* fire?"

Tekhne nodded. "Once the spell was cast, the gods stepped in to help ordinary humans have the abilities and power needed to complete the quests they were brought for."

"Gods-blessed," Arach whispered.

Tekhne nodded. "Precisely."

I glanced down, trying to reconcile the information with the body I was accustomed to. I didn't really feel any different than I had at home, but being able to manipulate fire was new.

I met Tekhne's eyes. "Did I switch places with someone or just get added to this world?"

The goddess shrugged. "I can't honestly say. There's a possibility you traded physical places with someone here to keep the balance of souls in each world."

"If I'm here, did the person I replaced go to my world?"

"That's a reasonable assumption."

"Oh sweet glory."

"What's wrong, Matsuko? This can't be all bad, can it?"

I swung around to look at Arach. "Do you remember how freaked out I was when I arrived in the jail? Imagine someone from this world ending up in mine with cars, airplanes, computers, and social media. They're likely to go insane."

He blinked. "None of those words made sense to me."

"Exactly. And this world isn't what I dreamed of when I thought of going on an adventure. I'd pictured something more like hiking in Banff or visiting the Incan temples in Mexico." I shot another look at Tekhne. "Why me? What was wrong with the other person I traded with? Weren't they a good enough champion?"

Tekhne shook their head. "We'll never know. You're here and they are not."

"That's not really a point in your favor."

The goddess shrugged. "Perhaps. But the spell brought us the people we needed and requested."

"We? Who's we?" I narrowed my eyes.

"Lord Ignius and I both endorsed you as our paladin. This is why you have an affinity for fire and music."

"So, you're hoping I'll find this Song Stone, and bring it back here. And then you'll do what with it? Use it to destroy Anima?"

Tekhne shook their head. "We don't want to destroy

her. She's our sister. We want to rehabilitate her. But we need the artifacts to help with that. We were holding her until we figured out how to make her better and that will only be possible with all the artifacts back together." The goddess strummed the vina. "Because of your skills in your own world, you are most suited to find my Song and bring it here so we may soothe her once more. But we must have your help to succeed."

I stared out at the land sweeping away from the temple on the hill and took a deep breath. Everything looked so soft with the green grass and I had the weird thought it would feel like velvet if I ran my hands over it.

It would make about as much sense as what I've been told.

I shook my head. "That's not right. Incorrect." I tried finding words other than the usual—crazy, insane, nuts, ridiculous. I'd been called all those things too many times because of my autism and I wasn't about to use them on someone else. "I'm not magical. I don't have power."

"All evidence to the contrary, m'dear." Arach chuckled and smoke drifted from his nostrils.

It must be a byproduct of being a dragon.

I'd never seen him actually smoking anything like a pipe or cigarette. I had seen him shift from the man who stood inside the temple with me to a large, scaly reptile with huge wings, a long tail, and a sinuous neck. The horns were pretty cool, too.

Focus.

"No, this doesn't make sense. Can someone please wake me up when it's all over?" I turned around to face the goddess with their vina and metallic lace outfit. "I can't be your champion. I don't know anything about fighting or magic or saving the world. I don't play D&D or the online games. I'm just me, an audiologist from Whidbey Island."

Tekhne laughed, the sound reminiscent of windchimes. "It wasn't the gods who brought you here, Matsuko. That was all a human effort. But now that you're here, we're offering the support of our power to return the world to its center and help heal our sister. And in exchange, we will send you home to your world."

I shook my head. "Wait. You say you'll let me go home if I help you. But if I don't somehow become this…" I trailed off and waved my hand. "Sorceress, magic-wielder, paladin person, I'll be stuck here forever?"

The goddess shrugged and chuckled. "It might not be as bad as that. The people here make beautiful music and art. And there are dragons." They winked as they inclined their head at Arach. Then their eyes narrowed and their face lost all its humanity. "But if you don't do this, this world will die, as will all its people—including you. Warmonger is working with something evil and is gaining power. He's using the Song Stone to push its power and the evil may well overtake your even own world."

"And you're saying that Anima's health is all that's keeping the world safe? That doesn't make any sense."

"No, I'm saying the artifacts protecting Anima have been stolen and now are being used to give evil a foothold here in this world."

"Artifacts? There were more than one stolen?"

The goddess nodded. "Yes, but you're only needed to find the Song Stone. Of course, you could refuse and live out your days doing nothing. But you'd have to stay here and watch the world crumble through your inaction. The choice is yours."

I barked an incredulous laugh. "No pressure or anything. And it's not much of a choice. Die fighting the evil unleashed in this world by someone else. Or die with everyone else when the evil gets around to this part of the world."

"Personally, if I'm going to die either way, I'd rather die fighting to save something." Arach shrugged, his words amused but his expression grave.

"Right." Fear surged in the back of my mind but I refused to let it out of its box.

Maybe the idiots who opened Anima's prison should've done the same.

I closed my eyes and swallowed hard. "Fine. I'll go on this quest for you. I'll learn magic and sorcery and whatever to save your world, and I'll bring back the Song Stone."

Tekhne tilted their head. "And what will you want in return for this effort?"

"I haven't decided yet. I guess what I want is all the choices when it's time. I'll do this and you'll pay whatever price I ask when I ask it. Deal?"

The goddess shot me a look full of rueful amusement. I'd heard that's what "grudging approval" looked like, but I wasn't the best at interpreting social cues from expressions.

"You're quite a negotiator, Matsuko, but you have yourself a deal. Now." Tekhne waved their hands. "It's time for you to go. May the Music flow and buoy your soul." They clapped two of their hands and the temple disappeared.

A soft grunt beside me told me Arach hadn't expected that mode of transportation either. I blinked. We stood in the center of a stone spiral in the velvety-green hills I'd seen from the temple. Twisting, I looked for the structure where we'd talked with Tekhne, but it appeared they'd sent us to some other valley.

"Remind me not to take the goddess's travel arrangements again. It's hell."

"Oh, you have no idea what's hell until you've tried to take a packed monorail train during rush hour." I shook my head. At least they hadn't landed us in the middle of some busy city street. "Where do you think Tekhne sent us?"

He lifted his head to smell the air. "Smells like one of the lakes in Aldmarsh. We'll probably see one on the other side of those ridges."

A trail disappeared into the rainy mists around our small valley, as if the sun punched a hole in the clouds, leaving us in a pool of light.

"So do we head for the lake?"

"You got any better ideas?" Arach raised an eyebrow.

I shook my head. "Nope."

"All right, then. I'll follow you."

CHAPTER FIVE

Arach

Tekhne's Temple had been located north of the Ribbon Rivers, a set of braided streams that wound their way through the high hills overlooking the sound between the mainland and the peninsula. But the goddess had sent us somewhere wetter and flatter than I'd been in a long time. Tall grasses rose to our waists as we tromped along the trail in the rainy mists.

This sucks bollocks.

I didn't mind being wet. I didn't mind being cold. But I hated being wet and cold, and this filled both descriptions.

Surprisingly, Matsuko said nothing, just kept plodding along with her hood up and her robes dragging in the wet. I couldn't imagine she was any less miserable, but she kept her own counsel and I'd found her expressions damn near impossible to read.

Another intriguing aspect about her. She'd do well in my father's court.

Not that I was thinking of introducing her to the rest of my problematic family. If my brothers didn't try to eat her or seduce her, my sisters would try to manipulate her against me or my father. And my father would ignore her for her humanity.

Fortunately, structures loomed out of the fog, and I could smell unwashed humanity and ale. Soon, light and sound filtered through the clinging mists and presented us with a decent sized village with humans dressed in heavy wool and boiled leather boots meant to keep out the damp. The clanging of a blacksmith's hammer sounded as we passed his forge and a blast of welcome heat made me sigh. I wished we could stop in front of the hot dry air, but I didn't think Matsuko would appreciate it despite her affinity for fire.

"There should be an inn or public house up ahead." I couldn't help but reassure her. She looked so dejected as she trudged through the mud of the main road and I wanted to give her hope. Which was the next on the long list of strange things I'd done in the last day or so.

Perhaps I'm coming down with something.

But my instincts were right as the local inn and pub came into view, appearing out of the fog like a welcome balm to our troubles. I grasped her elbow and steered her toward the doors just as two very large men stepped out into the roadway. Neither of them looked friendly or welcoming, and they had enough muscle mass on them to generate their own heat.

And their own stink.

I wrinkled my nose against their pungent aromas and wrapped my arm around Matsuko's waist to both help her when she stumbled but also to show the men she was with me. They eyed her with interest and didn't appear much bothered by my presence. I'd used my unassuming appearance to my advantage many times, but I wasn't in the mood for a fight and we ignored them as we slipped past.

The public house held more people inside than I expected, but with the weather I shouldn't have been surprised. No one really liked the damp cold, not even those who lived in it full time.

Thank the gods my home's to the south of this shite.

I strode up to the drinking counter and looked for the innkeeper. A portly man with the belly to fill out his stained apron eyed me and Matsuko warily, but he waddled over to see what I wanted when I waved a bit of silver.

"Whaddya want?"

"A good room, a hot meal for my companion and I, and a bath, in that order."

He shot a look at Matsuko and raised an eyebrow. "I ain't running a brothel. Take your bird elsewhere if ya want that."

"Insult my companion like that again, and you'll be pissin' blood for a week. Am I clear?" I put enough steel into my voice to make him swallow hard and nod quickly. His jowls flopped like a hound's.

"Right, then, gov'nor. Sorry, gov'nor. The room and meal and bath will cost ya two silvers, on account of heatin' and carryin' the water."

I narrowed my eyes and let him sweat as I considered. The price wasn't exorbitant, but I wanted him to second guess my willingness to pay for his dubious services.

"Let me see the room before I agree to such extravagance." Using my training as a prince let people see what they wanted to see. If they thought me someone of consequence, I usually got what I wanted.

He swallowed hard but bobbed his head in a jowly nod and barked something at one of the serving wenches as he trundled off up the stairs at the back of the establishment. I gestured to Matsuko to lead the way after him, but she had her attention on more of the big burly men who'd come through the door when we arrived.

"Best not to stare, love." I urged her with me as I followed the proprietor. "We don't want to draw more attention than is necessary before we're ready."

"Ready? Ready for what?"

"For whatever they plan to throw at us." I shrugged. More than likely, those big burly blackguards were part of the garrison to whichever lord held sway in Aldmarsh, and until we knew who we were up against, it was best not to catch their notice.

"They plan on throwing things at us?" She shot me a surprised look as I ushered her up the stairs.

"Let's hope not. The main point is, we don't know for whom they fight."

"Like Warmonger?"

"Hush." I hadn't meant it to come out so harshly, but I didn't want anyone to know Warmonger was our end goal. "We'll talk about it in the room where we have a modicum of privacy."

She didn't say anything more as we reached the floor above the public room. The sound was muted here and even the walls seemed sturdy. The innkeeper waited at the end of the hallway with a door open, wringing his hands as he shifted from foot to foot.

"Here's you go, gov'nor. Will it do, gov'nor?" The man's obsequiousness set my teeth on edge, but I strode past him into the room and looked around.

I was surprised. It was a large space with a real fireplace rather than a potbellied stove, and it had a wide, if not tall, bed. The room smelled clean and the rug covering the worn wood floor was plush. A small discreet chamber pot sat close to the window with diamond panes, and two oil lamps stood on bedside tables with lace doilies.

"It'll do. How much for a week?"

The man's eyes narrowed with calculation. "Will ye be requirin' a bath each night, m'lord?"

I shook my head. "No, just tonight."

"One gold Marshlin, 'twould be. Payable in advance."

I raised my chin and tilted my head. "Tell you what. Let us start with one night, the meal, and the bath for two silvers. If you exceed my expectations, I shall pay a full gold Marshlin for the rest of the time we stay."

"Very good, m'lord. I'd be honored, m'lord. What name shall I put on the reservation, like?"

"Lord and Lady Kamanzi of Wyvern's Edge."

"Very good, m'lord. Will ye be eatin' in the common room or up here in your lodgin'?" The innkeeper dug out the key to the door and handed it to me as he stared curiously at Matsuko, who had yet to remove her hood.

"We'll dine here in our room and there'll be a few coppers for you if you make it quick."

"Yes, m'lord. Of course, m'lord."

I herded the fat fool out the door and closed it on his bowing face before I turned to see what Matsuko had gotten up to. She'd moved to the bed and trailed her fingers along the embroidered coverlet. Despite its somewhat humble appearance, the embroidery showed elegant flowers in bright colors and made the room cheery despite the damp and dreary weather outside.

"He was annoying."

I barked a laugh. "Yes, he definitely was. Someone has laid a fire in the fireplace. Come sit by it and warm up while we wait for our supper."

"But how will you—"

Before she'd even finished her question, I'd lit the hearth with my breath and flooded the room with the welcoming light of the flames.

"Oh, right. I'm staying with a dragon prince." She shook her head but removed her boots and sat them near the door before settling on the chair I'd positioned in front of the hearth. "Thank you."

She rubbed her knees with her hands and I was struck at how beautiful they were. Long, delicate fingers with elegant nails showed the care she took of them, yet there was strength in the shape and musculature. I suddenly wanted those hands sliding over my body, following the lines of my muscles and wrapping around my cock.

I hissed in a breath and looked around for anything else to occupy my attention. Matsuko was a friend and travel companion. Perhaps even a battle buddy. She wasn't a possible bedding partner.

Unfortunately, my body and my mind couldn't agree and my gaze strayed back to her. She'd pushed off her hood and her glorious, long dark hair lay in a silken braid over one shoulder. She had a long slender neck that begged for soft kisses and small pert breasts that would fill each of my palms.

My cock stretched the fly of my trousers as my balls tightened up against its base, and I groaned, praying Matsuko wouldn't notice my unruly interest. Of course, I couldn't be that lucky.

"Are you all right, Arach?"

Her divine magical fragrance hit me just before the additional delicate floral scent filled my nose. My tongue stuck to the roof of my mouth as desire surged through me.

Why in the gods' names was I acting like a randy teenager at his first brothel?

"I'm…fine…" I growled the words and tightened my hands into fists to keep from grabbing her and rubbing my hard cock against her belly.

"You sound like you're in pain. Maybe you need the bath more than I do. Because the bath was for me, right? But I can let you have it. The fire is helping already."

Why was she still talking? And that scent, so damn beguiling. "No, no, I'll be fine. Internal furnace and all that."

Someone knocked on the door, thank the gods. "That'll be supper. Let's eat and worry about the bath after, yes?"

I spun away from her and tried to ignore her eyes on me. Instead, I focused on the serving wenches bringing up a small folding table and platters of food. It smelled surprisingly good and I hoped my appetite for nourishment would overtake the one for sexual pleasure. I smiled at the wenches and one of them winked at me. But no matter how lovely her creamy breasts were or how plump her ass, I couldn't get Matsuko's slim elegance out of my awareness.

"Thank you." I nodded to the women as they curtsied and the bawdy one winked again, sending me a sultry smile, but I closed the door on her without a thought.

"Looks like some sort of fish stew with steamed veggies and fresh dark bread." Matsuko had already pulled her chair over to the table and lifted the covers off the dishes. "Smells good. Can I serve you some?"

As long as you serve yourself up as the dessert course.

What in the name of the gods was wrong with me? I shook my head and wondered if I needed to run back out into the misty damp just to get myself back under control.

"Yes, thank you." It was the best I could do as I wrestled my cock into submission, and it didn't go gracefully.

She ladled the stew into a bowl and tore off a chunk of bread before setting them on the table for me. I loved her precise movements and the way she handled the dishes like an elegant dance. It was mesmerizing to watch.

"Where did you learn to serve food like that?" I dragged the other chair over and settled into it as she filled her own bowl.

One shoulder moved up and down in a shrug. "My grandmother. She was a stickler for proper table etiquette. She said if I could make the serving look like a graceful dance, it wouldn't matter what the food tasted like. Presentation was very important to her."

"It's magical. She was right."

Matsuko smiled at me, pleasure filling her expression and I was struck dumb at her beauty. Arching brows over her dark eyes spelled me more than any magic I'd encountered, but those full lips curling upwards at the edges were my downfall. They deserved to be kissed and often.

But the pleasure showing in her expression was all the reward I needed. It was addictive and made me want to compliment her more. I'd never wanted to please anyone as much as I wanted to please Matsuko. I was a prince and a thief—I was usually the one I wanted to please. But lately, life had turned as gray as the murky sky outside and I couldn't find any color or light, much less pleasure.

Bringing Matsuko pleasure made the whole room sparkle and the colors in the rug and coverlet on the bed brightened into jeweled tones.

"Enjoy." She tucked into her food and I sat there watching her, dumbstruck by my revelations and her beauty. She glanced up at me after she swallowed. "Aren't you going to eat?"

"Uh, yes. Yes of course."

The food was surprisingly good and hearty, and the bread complimented the stew. The roasted vegetables had been spiced with something savory and the whole meal brought great satisfaction.

Or the company does.

Just as we finished, there was a knock at the door. I left Matsuko gathering the dishes and stacking them neatly so the serving wenches could take them away. Outside in the hallway stood the proprietor's wife with two young men.

"Good e'enin', m'lord. Your bath?"

"Excellent. Please bring it in and set it in front of the fire."

The boys carried in a brass tub with high ends and set it in front of the fire. Then they picked up the dishes Matsuko had stacked and carried them out. Behind them came the women with pitchers of steaming water that they poured into the basin. It was impressive how smoothly they did the work and how quickly they filled it. On the way out, the serving woman who'd brought supper again winked at me as she passed, and I barely managed to keep myself from rolling my eyes.

"Just let us know when yer done, m'lord, and we'll clear away the bath." The older woman handed me some towels and two cakes of soap before she bobbed her head and stepped out to the hall. She curtsied and closed the door behind her.

I found Matsuko holding her hands above the steaming water, wiggling her fingers in the steam wafting off the tub. The yearning in her expression made me want to give her everything she needed.

"Go ahead and take your bath, Matsuko. I'll even help you wash your back if you wish."

"Okay." She turned to the bed and shrugged out of her outer robes.

At first I thought she'd be naked, but another dress filled in what the overcoat didn't cover. She tugged on the ties holding the dress tight to her body and then pulled it over her head. She wore a linen chemise under it that cupped her small pert breasts and my mouth dried as she lifted the garment off.

There she stood, all golden skin and lithe curves, with a triangle of dark hair over her mound, and my heart nearly leapt out of my chest.

That's not your heart, you nitwit.

My cock wasn't far behind and it strained against my fly, more excited than it had been before supper.

She slipped into the water with a soft hiss as the heat enclosed her and I swallowed a moan. When I agreed to help Matsuko, I hadn't expected her to be more than an interesting companion who'd entertain me for a while. And Lord Ignius knew she was extremely entertaining. But I also hadn't expected to be sexually attracted to her lovely body and her direct honest ways.

I stood transfixed as she leaned back and dunked her head to rinse her hair, her breasts popping up before her face broke the surface. Everything about her was elegance and grace, and I wanted to feel her body against mine. Without clothes. Preferably with erotic interactions.

As she began to scrub her hair with the soap cake, I cleared my throat and tried to find coherent words.

"Would you like some help with that?"

She raised her eyebrows. "You want to help me wash my hair?"

"I would drain the whole of Wandalup Bay to feel the silk of your hair against my skin."

She blinked. "What?"

I couldn't remember exactly what I'd said, but I wasn't about to repeat it.

"Yes, I'll help you wash your hair."

"Oh, okay, then." She extended the soap cake to me as I pulled one of the chairs over to the tub. "Please be thorough, but gentle. My hair is very thick."

I wet my hands in the bathwater, careful not to brush her skin, but I couldn't stop my gaze from her dusky nipples. Sweet gods and goddesses, I wanted to slide my hands over her breasts until those nipples tickled my palms and she moaned in pleasure. But I yanked my gaze back to the safer territory of her head as I lathered the cake in my hands.

Did I say it was safer? By the First Egg, I was so wrong.

Her wet hair was a heavy silken mass, so smooth I could barely believe it needed washing. But I was determined to make sure each glorious strand was clean by the time I was done. I dragged my fingers through the long fall of slippery darkness then rubbed the ends between my palms, making sure I'd soaped everything.

I loved the feeling of her hair in my hands especially when I picked up the little pitcher and poured warm water over the back of her head to rinse the soap out. It took multiple tries and I enjoyed every one of them. With the pitcher in one hand, went to work on her scalp with the other, occasionally adding a little water.

And she moaned.

I damn near dropped the pitcher as my fingers froze on her head.

“Are you well, Matsuko?”

“Um-hm. Don’t stop, please.”

Fuck me sideways, she was even polite when asking for pleasure. My cock hardened against my trousers and I swore my balls were turning blue. I took a deep breath and set the pitcher down as I used both hands to massage her scalp, trying to ignore the moans coming from her. Even if they turned me on more than most of the whores I’d visited throughout my life. I’d never wanted for female company, but I definitely wanted Matsuko.

And she’s your travel companion on a quest, numbskull!

I hurriedly finished massaging and poured the water over her head, shielding her eyes with one hand. I ignored the softness of her skin against my palm as I focused on rising her hair completely.

It’ll be over soon and then I can stop touching her.

Except I didn’t want to stop touching her. I wanted to caress in ways that would give us both pleasure and satisfaction. And normally, I’d have done that. I could’ve easily seduced my companion and spent the evening feasting on her magnificent body. But something about Matsuko made me think I’d be wiser to leave her be. Intimacy would be fun for one night, but the complications of our tryst would last a lifetime.

“There, I think I got all the soap out.”

“Thank you. That felt good.”

She nodded to me as she took the soap cake and worked on cleaning her body. I didn’t intend to watch as I had a lot to think about, but my gaze refused to stray away from her efficient motions. She didn’t waste time or efforts in cleaning her whole body, even going so far as to stand up in the tub and clean her pussy with nimble fingers.

Oh sweet gods!

I wanted those fingers to be mine. Or my tongue.

I gotta get out of here.

"Will you wash my back, please, Arach?"

Oh, now that wasn't fair. I swallowed hard and took the soap with a nod. I couldn't find the words to say anything. Now she wanted me to touch her body? I was so doomed.

I'd thought her hair was soft, but the slick skin of her back reminded me of the smoothest satin my sisters often bought for their gowns. I worried my fingers, rough from using weapons and lock picks, would scratch her and I made sure to finish her back quickly. My balls were definitely blue and my cock was like stone when I handed her back the soap.

"I'm going out."

"What? Why?" Matsuko rose, the water from the bath sluicing over her body and making my cock throb harder.

I turned my back and grabbed my cloak to keep the rain off. "I need some wine." *And some damn sanity.* "Lock the door behind me."

"But—"

I was out the door and along the hall before it had slammed shut, but I still kept going down the stairs, damn near slamming into a drunk guy who leaned too far into the opening.

"Oy! Watch where yer goin', ye numpty!"

I ignored him and wove my way through the noisy, smelly patrons to the door. I had to get out of there before the subtle floral scent of Matsuko's skin overwhelmed my good sense and forced me to seduce her into bed. She was my friend and my travel companion, not my lover!

But what if she could be your lover? What if she could be your mate?

Oh, for the love of the First Egg, that was absurd.

I broke into a run despite the spitting rain and the dark,

slippery street. I had to get out of town and shift so I could clear my head. But visions of Matsuko, naked and dripping, filled my mind's eyes, and my dragon half growled with desperate desire. I wanted Matsuko naked and moaning beneath me more than I'd ever wanted anything, including the hoard I had stashed away in a secret location. I would've given away the whole thing to have her as my lover and mate.

What the hell is wrong with me?

I made it to the end of the buildings looming out of the fog and leapt into the misty air, shifting on the fly. I needed a fucking cold bath or a dunking in a frozen lake. Anything to cool the desire and need burning through me. Considering I was a dragon and naturally ran hot, that was saying something.

My wings snapped downward and shot me high above the trees. I pumped them hard to escape the roaring need riding me like an addiction. I sped through the thick, wet clouds, hoping to find relief or sanity—whichever hit me first.

I flew high enough to break through the clouds and enter the still air of the night sky where only the moon and stars kept me company. I took a deep breath and stretched my wings out to glide, trying to calm my thundering heart and my aching cock. While it didn't show in my natural form like it did in my human disguise, it still throbbed with desperate need of relief.

Matsuko. Her name echoed through my mind and turned my world upside down. How could one human woman, a sorceress of song and flame, disrupt a dragon's life and well-being? She was gods-touched and a champion for them, but she was still human. How could a dragon, a being so long lived and magical, find attraction, connection, and pleasure with a human?

But your life was gray before she arrived.

The voice came out of nowhere and I growled in

response. I hated that it was right. I'd been in a rut before I met my sorceress no more than two days earlier. And I'd been hiding in prison just to get some rest. Life had been boring. The same tricks to steal the same baubles from the same idiots. No variation. No excitement. No color. Just dull sameness, day after day, year after year, decade after decade.

Until Matsuko.

I'd told her earlier that she was a treasure and an oddity, but in reality, she was more precious than that. She was a being that made me laugh, told me straight up how she saw things, and didn't hide behind sweet words or devious actions. She was guileless, and yet not as naïve as I'd first thought. She didn't know this world, but she'd learned fast and accepted her role in it despite her fear and lack of understanding.

Not even my father would've been willing to do something so daring.

And she has no one to protect her or teach her but you.

I glanced down and realized the clouds had petered out above rolling hills. Craggy peaks showed in the distance and the marshes had disappeared. I pivoted in the sky and flew back toward the little village and the rainstorm seated over it as I mulled over my companion and my desires.

I wanted Matsuko as more than just a travel companion, magical pupil, or friend. I wanted her as my lover, protector of my soft dragon's heart, and my mate. But she was bound to head back to her own world—a world I knew less about than she knew of mine. What would happen if I gave her my heart and she left me?

I keened a cry of pain that startled a flock of geese using the storm to disguise their migration and I considered chasing them for a little distraction. But I'd left Matsuko alone in our room, in a village neither of us knew, with limited knowledge of this world. Not my wisest move.

I descended through the clouds, inhaling the scents to

navigate through the fog. I didn't want to hit any trees in a forest or buildings of the village. And I didn't want to run into any wizards' towers or overlords' castles. That would just be bad.

Nothing quite so sexy as a dragon running into someone's house.

So I listened and scented and felt the currents of air to determine where everything was located in the mists. I got lucky and made it to the edge of the village before shifting into my human disguise. It always felt like stuffing myself into pants that were just a little too tight and stuffing cotton in my ears and nose. But I dropped to the muddy road and shook myself until my dragon self fit somewhat comfortably into my human form.

I'd just stepped up to the first building when I heard heavy footsteps slurping in the mud ahead. I ducked into the shadowed darkness of a recessed doorway and watched who came by.

A troop of the big, hulking men in leather and metal armor slogged through the mud, headed out of town. They all wore some sort of insignia on their chests, but with the mist and the darkness, even my excellent eyesight couldn't pick it up. They weren't speaking, which was unusual for soldiers or mercenaries of any company, and they moved past me without a look either left or right.

I guess when you're the baddest bastards on the road, you don't worry for much.

I could've taken them all out without much effort, but my goal was to get back to Matsuko. Still, it was curious that these men made no small talk.

Once they'd passed, I did my best to make it back to the inn quickly despite the thick, sucking mud and the damp rain. It was late and most of the revelers had gone home, but a few hardy souls slumped in the corners, drinking away their sorrows. I would've joined them except I wanted to get back to Matsuko. She could protect herself, but her efforts would likely take down the inn as well as her attackers.

I didn't see the proprietors on my way up, but the serving wench caught my eye as I went through the public room and smiled suggestively.

Fire and scale, that woman never gives up.

I didn't bother to smile as I headed up the stairs and down the hallway to our room. I had no idea how long I'd been gone, but Matsuko had extinguished the lamps when I unlocked the door.

The fire still burned in the hearth and kept out the wet chill trying to get through the diamond-paned window. I focused on the fire, adding another log, and banking it so it would burn all night. The room remained toasty and I didn't want Matsuko getting cold.

That's my story and I'm sticking to it.

Taking a deep breath, I finally shot a look at the bed. Matsuko lay on her side facing the wall with the covers pulled all the way up to her head. I mourned not being able to see what she choose the bed down in, but it was probably safer that way. Lord Ignius knew I would've been challenged to keep my hands off her more intimate parts.

I would eventually have to find the balance between my burning desire for her and protecting my heart from a loss I wasn't sure I could recover from. Dragons were usually impervious to romance and emotional connections. Especially the dragons in the Uzekamanzi family line. But once a dragon gave their heart to someone, it was given without ways of getting it back.

I pulled off my boots and set them beside the door, dismayed that I'd left mud on the floor in my room. I remember Matsuko taking hers off immediately and realized she'd done it to keep the floors clear of debris. I grimaced and slunk back to rug in front of the fire. The tub and the table had been removed, so there was plenty of space to stretch out on the floor.

I pulled the extra blanket off the foot of the bed and used my damp cloak as a pillow as I settled my ass on the floor. It wasn't the nastiest place I'd slept—hell, the last few nights in the Wyvern's Edge jail had been worse—but I would've preferred the bed I'd paid for. And the woman in it.

Therein lies a path to destruction.

But I feared I'd already taken the first steps anyway.

CHAPTER SIX

Matsuko

Morning came with lighter gray light than the day before and the scent of something rich, like coffee but with more spices in it. I turned over to see what had become of Arach and found him sitting at the returned folding table and chairs in front of a crackling fire. He held a book in his hands as he sipped from a thick mug. A pottery pitcher steamed beside him on the table.

As much as I wanted to get up and inspect the hot drink, I didn't want to move from under the warm blankets on the bed. It had been my curse of mornings. The warmth and silence of rest made me hesitate to reenter the world of light, noise, motion, and stimulation that always awaited me. But nothing ever got done by lying in bed and I had a job I'd promised to do.

Plus there's coffee.

Sighing heavily, I pushed my way out of the blankets and moved across the floor to the other chair opposite Arach.

"Good morning."

I grunted my acknowledgment, which made him smirk,

and poured myself a mug of the fragrant hot liquid. Then I slumped into the chair beside the fire and tried to find my coherency in my jumbled thoughts. One thing came clear. He'd ducked out at the end of my bath, but I didn't know why. Had I done something to make him bolt? He'd been nervous, but I couldn't fathom the reason.

"Are you okay?" I met his gaze and his amber eyes widened.

"Yes, I'm fine. Why?"

I shrugged. "You ran out last night like your tail was on fire. Did you get your wine?"

He blinked as if trying to decipher what I meant. I frowned. Hadn't he said he was going out for wine? It hadn't made sense at the time, considering we could have asked the innkeeper. But I assumed he wanted to choose his own bottle from the bar downstairs and expected to find him hungover this morning.

But he sat there drinking his coffee and reading his book without a care in the world.

"Oh, uh, no, I didn't get the wine. I decided to go for a flight."

"In the rain?" I raised my eyebrow. That sounded like complete lunacy given how miserable the weather had been. Why wouldn't he have wanted to stay in the warm, dry room with me?

Oh.

I'd been in the room, naked, and he'd been nervous. Maybe I'd offended him by washing in front of him. Maybe nudity was a taboo here. It certainly was for women in my world. Maybe he'd found my body repulsive. I had no idea what dragons found proper or attractive, but I'd be sure to ask for a privacy screen or something next time I wanted to bathe.

"Oh, I see. I'm sorry."

Arach blinked. "For what are you apologizing, Matsuko?"

"For offending you. I'll be more careful next time."

He laughed. "I'm not offended. Why would you suggest such a thing?"

His amusement pissed me off. Was he laughing at me with derision or pity? Just because I didn't understand his customs didn't mean he could make fun of me for it. It wasn't my fault this whole damn world was new to me, and the rules had changed.

"Because you ran out of here like someone had lit your ass on fire. Because you were afraid to touch me. Because every time you looked in my direction, you'd grimace and look away." I scowled at him. "I might not react like neurotypical people to unspoken cues, but I do notice and see them and analyze them. What I interpreted was you'd rather spend the night in the rain than see me naked. Next time, do me a favor and just get a second room."

I set my mug down despite the delicious flavor of the hot drink and rose, intending to find my hopefully dry robes and put them on before he had to stare at my physical hideousness all morning. I discovered they'd been folded over the door of the wardrobe beside the window and they'd been cleaned.

I dragged the dress over my head, struggling to get my arms into the sleeves and my head through the collar. I yanked it down, pulling strands of hair out of the braid I'd woven the night before, and that irritated me even more. Heat rose in my face and hands, and they started to glow with blue light.

Oh, for fuck's sake, not now.

The last thing I wanted to do was set the inn on fire. I started to hum to bring my emotions under control, but my anger fanned the flames, and the glow grew brighter. "Clocks" by Coldplay filled my head and I closed my eyes, trying to let the music settle my jumbled emotions. I was so much more susceptible to emotional storms in this world, but I chalked it up to not knowing the rules of social engagement like I did in my own world. I had safeguards and routines there, but it was like the Wild West here.

"Deep breaths and listen to the music, Matsuko." Arach's voice intruded just before his hands grasped my arms in a gentle grip. "You have more control than you believe. Focus on where you want the energy to go, what you want it to do. You control it."

"I don't know if I can."

"Believe you can."

"I have no experience controlling it. I don't know how."

"It's not about experience, Matsuko, it's about belief. Believe the energy, the magic will do what you want when you want it. See it in your mind's eye and believe you can manipulate it any way you want to." He held my shoulders and pressed his chest up against my back, giving me a steady backboard on which to lean.

Clenching my jaw, I took a deep breath like he said and imagined what I wanted the magical energy to do. Not flames this time, but a slow fade into quiescence with the extras popping off harmlessly into the air like colorful bubbles. I could see each delicate sphere in marbled jewel tones floating up toward the ceiling and popping with the tinkling of chimes.

Arach laughed behind me and I opened my eyes to see what I'd envisioned actually happen. The bubbles of magic floated up to the ceiling and broke in shards of sound. They were beautiful and I watched them with wonder.

"Well done. Excellent first step to controlling your magic, Matsuko." He turned me around to look me in the eyes. "And I didn't run out of here because I didn't want to spend the night with you. I retreated because I was feeling too much sexual attraction toward you and I didn't know what to make of it. I also didn't know how you'd feel about it and until I could come to terms with it on my own, I didn't want to toss it at you."

"Oh." I stared at him, trying to decipher if he meant his words or was making fun of me. "So you're sexually attracted to me?"

"More than I ever expected."

I narrowed my eyes. "What does that mean?"

"It means that I knew you were intriguing from the moment I met you."

"Yes, I remember. A treasure and an oddity."

He grimaced. "Yes, a poor choice of words on my part, for which I'm very sorry and will be more clear from now on." He drew me back to the table and handed me my mug, the coffee-like drink still warm. He sat down across from me and rubbed the back of his neck, an odd expression of discomfort on his handsome face. "You undressed and got into the bath in front of me. Then you asked me to help you wash your hair and your back."

I frowned. "Yes, I needed help. Why did this scare you?"

"Because I found myself wanting to do more than just wash your hair or back, and I hadn't intended to seduce you. In the dragon world—in *my* world—bathing or grooming someone is often a prelude to sexual activities to relieve stress and give pleasure." He rubbed his thumbs over the edges of his mug. "We hadn't discussed what that meant before you bathed, and I hadn't expected to want to be more than your travel and quest companion."

I tried to interpret what he was actually saying under all the details. "Are you saying you want me, but you don't want to want me?"

He smiled in relief. "Yes, exactly."

"So wanting me sexually is a bad thing?" I'd already experienced the difficulties of finding someone who liked me in my own world. Now I was being snubbed in this one.

"What? No, this is not a bad thing."

"Which? The wanting me sexually or the wanting to want me?"

He blinked and frowned. “I don’t understand.”

“Neither do I! Which is it, Arach? Do you want me sexually or not?”

“Yes, I want you. I’ve wanted you since you threatened to light me on fire.”

I stopped and looked at him. “You’re really strange.”

He laughed. “I’m not going to argue with you there. But I would like to clear something up if you’re willing to talk about it.”

“Okay. What?” I sipped my coffee to settle a little and waited him out.

“Would you be amenable to sharing intimacies for the duration of our quest?”

I stared at him a long time as I tried to figure out what he was really asking, and it occurred to me he used big words when he was nervous.

Arach is nervous?

It seemed totally out of character for what little I knew about him, but I didn’t know him that well and maybe sex was a taboo subject among dragons.

“Just so I’m clear, you’re asking if I want to have sex with you while we’re together for the quest?”

“Yes, exactly.”

I nodded. “What about after?”

“After? You mean once we find the Song Stone and return it to the goddess’s temple?”

“Yes, after that.”

He grimaced and shrugged, not quite meeting my gaze. “I assume you’ll go home. Won’t you?”

Home. I hadn’t thought that far ahead, mostly because I rarely saw beyond the present moment. It had frustrated my siblings and parents that I was always focused on the present and never planned more than a few steps or activities. I suspected it would frustrate Arach, too. And the whole goal of finding the artifact to keep a goddess asleep was to get back home to my world. Wasn’t it?

"I don't know. Do we know if Tekhne has the abilities to send me back or were they just trying to get me to do this for them and I'll be shit-outta-luck later?"

He paused and tilted his head. "Do you want to go home to your world?"

I dropped my gaze to my hands. My home world was familiar and my routines were comfortable. I didn't have to worry about too much happening outside my experience. I had my practice, my clients, my family, and a few friends. I even had a beta fish that at least tolerated me. The patterns and pathways of my life didn't deviate much, and I usually preferred it. I always thought it was what I needed. I needed the routines and consistency. That was what my teachers and family members had told me, and I believed them.

Being there with Arach, and magic, and walking, talking goddesses was scary, off-balance, ever-changing, and inconsistent. But I was learning new skills and people depended upon me to complete a task, however impossible it sounded. They had expectations and I had my own. I'd never not completed a task given to me.

But eventually, we'd finish the quest and I'd have to make a decision.

I lifted my gaze and squared my shoulders. "I don't know. I don't have enough data yet to make an informed decision."

"What's this 'data'?"

I blinked. "Oh, uh…it's another way of saying statistical information."

He raised an eyebrow. "You don't have enough information to make a decision about wanting to go home?"

"No, I don't. I need more experience to weigh the cost-benefit analysis."

He slowly shook his head. "You are truly one of the most extraordinary people I have ever met, and so very beautiful in your uniqueness. But my original question stands, would you like to have sex with me, repeatedly, while we are on this quest together?"

"Yes."

He blinked. "That's it? Just yes?"

I frowned. "Is there another answer you're looking for?"

"No, no, I just have never had someone answer so simply."

"It was a direct yes or no question, and my answer is yes." I swallowed some more coffee. "But what about after the quest ends? Will you still want to have sex with me then?"

A warm smirk curled his lips as he reached across the table to brush his fingers across my cheek. "I don't think there will ever come a time when I don't want to have sex with you, Matsuko."

His touch and his expression made my chest heat up and I had the strangest urge to laugh. But I didn't want him to think I laughed at him so I grasped his hand and turned my face to kiss his palm. He gasped and his eyes widened as he growled low in his chest. It was an erotic sound and it made me shiver.

"Are you okay, Arach?"

"No, 'okay' doesn't begin to cover how I feel." He rose from his seat and his trousers tented around his erection. "I'm more than okay. It would be accurate to say I'm aroused and very interested in taking you to bed right now. Would you like me to make love to you right now?"

I swallowed hard as excitement built in my chest. "Yes, I would like that very much."

"Excellent answer."

He grasped my hand and pulled me up into his arms. "I know you just put this on, but can we take it off again? I'd very much like to see you naked."

I frowned. "Didn't you see me naked last night?"

"Oh yes, and it was the most unbearable moments of my life. But I didn't get to look *and* touch, and I'd very much like to do that now, *sheshtana*." He helped tug the dress over my head and tossed it to the side. "There's something very sexy about you wearing this chemise. It shows just enough to let my imagination run wild."

I tilted my head. "Even if you've seen me naked?"

"Even so. It lets me remember and get excited all over again." He kissed my neck and shoulder as he slowly gathered the skirt of the chemise in his hands, revealing my legs. "I want to run my hands over every inch of your golden skin and find out where the textures change from silken to satin to smooth."

The fluttery feeling grew in my belly and my pussy tightened up with preparation for…something. I'd had sex before, but I'd only felt those sensations a handful of times. In most of my sexual encounters, the men hadn't made much effort to make me excited. I'd been wet, lubricated for their penetration, but not really excited or interested.

But Arach's touches made my skin grow hot and sensitive, and my nipples hardened to little points against the bodice of the chemise. And his hands on my thighs under the cloth tickled with erotic pleasure. He trailed his fingers over my skin until he reached my buttocks, then he squeezed the muscles there as he groaned.

"I love the feel of your ass in my hands, Matsuko." He squeezed them again. "Let me take this chemise off you so I can look at you fully."

I nodded, but stopped him before he lifted the cloth over my head. "I have two questions first."

Arach paused and tilted his head. "What are those, *sheshtana*?"

"Okay, three questions. The first is, what does 'sheshtana' mean?"

"It's a term of endearment in the dragon language. Something akin to sweetheart or darling. Don't you like it?"

I tilted my head and let the word sift around my awareness. The word had qualities of warmth and desire without being cloying. I met his gaze and nodded. "I like it."

He smirked. "And your other questions?"

"Are you going to get undressed?"

He chuckled. "Would you like me to?"

"Yes, I want to see you naked, too."

"Very well." He stepped back and tugged at the frilly necktie-looking thing at his throat. "I shall undress. What's your third question?"

Watching him take his clothes of was surprisingly erotic. He wasn't trying to be sexy, but the slow reveal of his pale skin the color of the beach sand on Lake Washington made my stomach flutter and my vagina tighten with anticipation. A subtle pattern showed on his skin as he turned in the dim light, like the brocade cloth my mother used for our fancy clothes for holidays. I wanted to look closer, and when his trousers came off, I definitely needed a closer look.

"Better?" He set his clothing aside and turned to face me.

"Yes, much better." I nodded, my gaze locked on his groin. "Do you want me to take off the chemise?"

"Oh, no. That's my job, sheshtana." He smiled as he strode toward me, his penis growing harder as I watched. "I want to reveal all your soft skin like opening a gift."

Normally, words didn't mean much more than their face value, but when Arach used them in his sultry voice with that intense look in his eyes, they took on more meaning. I could hear his desire and interest in the way he said the words and it made my stomach flutter again.

He tugged the chemise up once more and exposed both my legs and my mound. I usually kept the hair trimmed, but since it had been awhile and I was in a new world, the pubic hair had grown to its normal width and length. Arach didn't seem to mind as he stroked his fingers through it and brushed my vulva. My vagina tightened with the sensation and I gasped in pleasure.

"You smell delicious, Matsuko." He pulled the chemise completely off and tossed it aside as his gaze fastened on my breasts. "And your breasts are beautiful. The perfect fullness on your lithe body." He cupped them, gently strumming the nipples with his thumbs. "But you didn't answer my question."

I blinked. He'd asked me another question? I tried to think back through the conversation, but his touches derailed my memory train.

"Question?"

"Yes, it seems we both have them. What is your third question?"

Oh, right, I did have three questions, but the third one had fluttered out the window the moment he touched me. I tried hard to focus on what I'd wanted to ask as he bent down and sucked on my nipples, but my mind didn't want to think.

"I've forgotten and I'm not convinced it was important anyway."

He rumbled a laugh as he rose to his full height and drew me back to the bed. "Perhaps you'll remember later. At the moment, though, I'd prefer you just feel instead of think. Let me…" He stopped and met my gaze with molten amber eyes. "May I pleasure you?"

No one had ever asked me that before. It was always implied but not flat-out asked. But Arach didn't leave anything to chance and his direct communication settled some of the built-up uncertainty. He wanted my permission and he didn't want to guess that he had it.

"Yes, please. Pleasure me, Arach."

He growled and laid me on the bed where he crawled over me with his hard erection hanging below his body like an erotic exclamation point. I wondered if he punctuated all his thrusts like a hard stop at the end of a sentence, but I closed my lips before the absurd notion burst out. I sort of expected him to fall on me like a starving beast, but Arach constantly surprised me as he paused to inhale the scent between my legs before kissing and licking his way back up to my breasts.

"I'm very tempted to taste you, Matsuko."

I raised an eyebrow. "I'm sure that's a normally sexy statement, but coming from a dragon, it's a little unnerving."

Arach paused and blinked at me, then threw his head back with a loud laugh. "Yes, I see your point. What I meant, though, is I want to taste your lovely pussy and make you come so hard you see stars and call my name."

"Is that even possible?" When he raised his eyebrows, I added. "The seeing stars part, not the name part."

The sultry smirk was back on his lips. "Perhaps we'll test it to find out, yes? But not today. I want to pleasure you with my cock and watch your release take over your whole body."

I wasn't sure how he'd do that if he was the one making love with me, but he reached between my legs and rubbed the folds of my vulva with practiced motions, making me gasp. He growled in a rhythmic cadence that almost sounded like a purr and it built up my arousal even more than his touches.

"Do you feel my fingers caressing your pussy, Matsuko?"

"Y-yes."

"This is where I'm going to slide my cock." His fingers dipped inside my opening, teasing the walls of my vagina with light strokes. "I'm fairly large so I want to get you as warmed up as I can before I push my shaft inside you." His glowing amber eyes held mine as he rocked his hand in time with this finger thrusts. "I can feel you getting so wet for me and your sweet cream is coating my hand."

He pulled his hand away from my vulva and I made an involuntary sound of protest, still rocking my hips in hopes he'd return to pleasuring me. His eyes gleamed as he licked my juices off his fingers while rubbing his penis and testicles against my wet mound.

"Patience, my lovely sorceress. I just wanted a little taste before I take you." His eyes closed as he savored the flavor of my cream. "Oh, you are divine ambrosia. I see I'll need to sample your sweetness firsthand next time we do this. And there will definitely be a next time."

"Good, because the way you make me feel is something I want to repeat." I sounded breathless, but the need for more of the sensations he gave me increased.

He chuckled as he returned his hand to my groin. "I'm glad to hear this." He grasped his penis and rubbed the tip against my vulva, spending spikes of hot pleasure straight through me. "I just have one question before I slide my cock into your honeypot."

"What question?"

"Have you had sex before, or are you a virgin?"

I moaned and rocked my hips to get closer to the hard heat of him, but he held himself just far enough away as he waited for my answer.

"That's actually two questions, but yes, I've had sex before, so no, I'm not a virgin."

"Oh, thank the gods." He lined up his penis and thrust it deeply into my vagina.

We both groaned as he came to a stop buried completely to the hilt with his hips resting in the cradle of mine. I had never felt so full and so aroused in my life, and I both wanted him to stay where he was and move as need took over my awareness. I liked having him in my body, his hot hardness filling me up completely. But I also wanted him to move, to drag that fullness out and thrust it back in to build the friction. There was no logic in the conflicting emotions, just pure desire for more of something.

"Are you well, Matsuko?" Arach held himself rigid while his penis filled me and sweat slid down his temples as he waited for my answer

"No."

He blinked in shocked surprise. "No?"

"No, I need you to move. Now." I grabbed his beautiful buttocks and held on as I rocked my hips to pull him impossibly closer.

He grunted and grinned, then pulled his hips back before plunging back into my slick vagina. The friction building between us electrified nerves I'd never experienced before and made me want more. More thrust, more pressure, more speed. Just more. I lost all coherency in the wash of pleasure, but Arach seemed to know what I needed because he sped up and thrust harder, increasing the friction.

A new sensation started, one that had been elusive in my old life. It felt like a combination of anticipation, warmth, need, and eroticism all rolled into one, and building faster than I could analyze it. I whimpered and writhed under Arach's exertions and loved the feeling of him slamming into me faster and harder than ever. The surge of the new feeling built beyond my ability to contain it and when it broke over me, I cried out, overwhelmed by the elation and exaltation and pleasure that filled my whole being.

Arach must have been in a similar state, because he stiffened above me and his penis felt even larger in my vagina than it did before. He gave me three more thrusts before he let out a growling snarl and bent forward to sink very sharp teeth into my shoulder. I jerked in surprise, but instead of pain, the pleasure returned stronger than before and I was swept into another orgasm as he slowly rocked his shaft in me.

At last, he released my shoulder and licked it a couple of times as if soothing the minuscule hurt before dropping his head beside mine while keeping his weight on his arms. We both rested there for a few moments, trying to catch our breaths. I'd never felt anything like it in past sexual encounters, and I suddenly understood why much of the human population seemed obsessed with sex.

If they're always chasing that feeling it makes sense. I definitely want more.

CHAPTER SEVEN

Matsuko

Arach still hadn't moved and his penis remained in my vagina. I found I didn't want him to leave just yet. But his silence made me nervous. Had I pleased him as much as he pleased me? Did he like what we'd done? My sexual resumé wasn't extensive and I'd rarely wondered how my partners felt about our actions. Usually because they'd said something like, "Thanks, babe, liked it." But Arach hadn't said anything and the longer his silence continued, the more uncertain I became.

"Are you okay, Arach?" My voice sounded hesitant, and it frustrated me to be so unsure.

"Yes, yes, I'm more than okay. I'm just trying to catch my breath while I give my cock a chance to relax and come to terms with what we've done."

While that sentence could have meant just coming to terms with sex, there was a quality to his statement that made me think there was more to it than that. But first question first.

"Your penis takes time to relax?" I'd never heard of such a thing, but Arach was the first dragon I'd made love with so this was all new to me.

"Yes. It's called the Love Anchor among my people and when a male comes in his…partner, his cock expands into a sort of knot or bulge to keep him lodged in her until their emotional connection can be established."

I frowned. "That's rather inconvenient for casual sex, isn't it?"

He chuckled tiredly. "Very. But it doesn't happen with casual sex. It only happens when the dragon male finds a most rare and precious connection. Then he feels the urge to bite his partner to seal their bond and share their auras, establishing their lifelong relationship."

I sifted through his words, trying to understand the meanings of them in their given configuration. "You bit me at the end."

"Yes, I did."

I took a few more moments to understand the implications. "Does that mean you're bound to me for all your life?"

"Yeeeppp." He drew the word out on a long sigh. "And you're bound to me."

I considered some more. "Even if I'm not a dragon myself?"

He raised his head to meet my gaze. "In terms of experience, I'm just as new at this as you, but it appears that I can bond with someone who's not a dragon because I managed to do it with you." He bit his lip and unease filtered into his expression. "I recognize this might cause some issues with regards to your return to your own world, and I want you to know I hadn't intended to mate with you for life."

"You were more expecting to do casual sex, right?"

"Yes, exactly. Well, perhaps not casual, but definitely not binding."

I bit my bottom lip. "Are you sorry you bonded with me?"

His penis finally relaxed enough to slip out of my body and he rolled to my side, but propped himself up on his elbow to keep eye contact.

"This is a two-pronged answer, so if you give me the time, I will explain both to you, all right?"

I nodded. "But you will explain it clearly?"

"Yes."

I took a deep breath. "Okay."

"Very well." He found the end of my braid and smoothed it against my breast. "I'm sorry I bonded with you because I don't want you to suffer if you choose to go back to your world. I have no idea how the bond works—I've never done it with anyone else—and I don't know how it will work in another world. The last thing I want to do is make things difficult for you."

He slid his hand down my body to rub his fingers through my wet vulva, sparking more of those fluttery feelings in my belly. "But I wanted you from the moment I met you and you're someone special. I knew that immediately. While I didn't plan to mate with you and I wouldn't have chosen to do it so soon, I'm not unhappy we've bonded through sex. And I'm more than happy to spend more time perfecting our sexual interaction anytime you're interested."

"So you're happy to be bonded to me here in this world?" I needed to be clear.

"Yes, very happy."

"Even though I have no magical skills, I haven't been here longer than two or three days, and I might be going home to another world?" When I put all the things close together, it sounded farfetched at best.

"That's truly a risk, but I wouldn't change anything." He grinned. "My life has been an adventure since I left home and made my own way in the world. My father and sibs weren't pleased with me, but what did they need another dragon prince around for, anyway?"

He shrugged though I could feel some of his sadness, which was strange because I'd never felt any of his emotions before.

"I've been choosing my own path for over a half a century and I'm not about to stop now. You're the family I've chosen, not the one I inherited."

I tilted my head. "You've been on your own for over fifty years?"

"Of course. I turned a hundred and twenty-six in the spring this year." He smiled at my wide eyes. "Why? How old are you?"

I'd been told no one was supposed to ask my age as it was rude. But no matter what age I was, I'd never be older than Arach.

"Thirty-three in August, or late summer or whichever."

"You wear it beautifully and I'd be happy to show you my appreciation again." He kissed the side of my neck below my ear and I wiggled from the ticklishness.

"No, I'm hungry. Will breakfast be brought or do we have to go out to find it?"

Before he could answer, there was a knock on the door. We both shot a look at the solid wooden portal.

"If ye want another night, pay up. Otherwise, be on yer way by the eleventh hour." The rough male voice didn't sound like he cared one way or the other. Definitely not the proprietor we'd met the night before.

Arach turned his attention back to me. "Shall we stay here for a bit longer or find other accommodations?"

"I don't know. Do you think staying here will help us find what we're looking for, or set us up to be caught by those who already have it?" I sat up and rested my arms on my knees. "Last night, those big hulking guards were hanging around the common room and they could be part of Warmonger's garrison of soldiers. But if they're hanging out here in the common room, that's not much distance from them when we get what we're looking for."

Arach nodded and rolled off the bed, presenting me with his lovely patterned ass to enjoy. He had beautiful musculature and I enjoyed every moment he allowed me to stare at it. He caught me staring when he turned around with his shirt in his hands. I hadn't noticed earlier but the pattern around his groin was darker and the scales looked larger, as if mimicking where pubic hair would be. Even without hair, I liked looking at his penis and testicles, and I wanted more opportunities to touch them.

As if he'd heard my thought, his penis began to flex and harden, and his sultry smirk returned to his face.

"See something you like, sheshtana?"

To my surprise, I laughed. "Yes, every time. I look at you because I like you. And I like your body, and I want to play with your penis next time."

He jerked his shirt over his head and grinned. "I'd be honored to have you play with my cock. But first, let's get our things together and find other lodgings. Your concerns are valid and in our case, wise."

"Yes, okay, good plan."

I slid out of the bed and found my chemise and dress, trying not the cringe at wearing them again without a wash. I pulled the chemise over my head and wondered what I would wear if I had to wash all my clothes. That thought expanded into shopping for new clothes and cleaning supplies and food and another place to sleep, and my forward motion ground to a stop.

"Matsuko, are you still with me?"

I blinked and looked up at a fully dressed Arach with our bag of random supplies over his shoulder.

"What?"

"I said, we'll get something on the way out of the village. Are you all right?"

"Oh, yes." I dragged my dress on then reached for my overcoat and socks. "These are nasty." But what choice did I have? The boots would give me blisters without them.

"I'd like to find some different clothes to wear."

"Different?"

"Yes, preferably pants with pockets, and clean. Socks and a few long-sleeved shirts." I met his surprised gaze. "What? Aren't those the kinds of clothes you want to wear?"

"Yes, but I'm male."

"What does that have to do with anything?" I snorted as I stuffed my feet back into the socks. They weren't very comfortable. "Pants keep my legs warm and dry when traveling, and clean socks are a blessings. No blisters."

I laced up my boots and shrugged into my overcoat, buttoning up the top and raising the hood. "Okay, I'm ready."

Arach nodded and opened the door to the hallway. He paused and glanced toward the stairs before ushering me out into the hall. Sounds filtered up from the public room, but only a few voices instead of a raucous rush. I closed the door behind me and followed him downstairs, keeping the hood low over my eyes. I didn't want the people in this village to remember me beyond being Arach's companion.

"Right, then, you leavin', m'lord?" The portly proprietor kept shooting looks in my direction.

"Yes, we've chosen to move on." He wisely didn't say more.

"Well, then. Fair journey to you and your lady."

Again, the man tried to get a good look at my face, but I turned my head to look toward the door. Sunlight showed through the open portal and a light breeze freshened the stale air. I turned my feet toward it in preparation for an easy escape. The hair on the back of my neck rose the longer we stood there talking to the owner and my stomach cramped.

That's just because I'm hungry.

But I couldn't ignore the itch between my shoulder blades. I'd had the same feeling as a young girl when my father's uncle would come to visit us. He was old and to be respected, but he'd stare at me with an intense expression, like he wanted something, and my stomach would cramp so badly I'd double over in pain.

The pain wasn't present, but the unease and warning blared in the back of my mind.

Arach finally finished speaking and escorted me out into the sunlit day. Some of the unease lifted, but I remained on edge. Logic said I shouldn't have been nervous, but my gut was smarter than my mind in many cases, and I'd learned to listen to it.

He sniffed the air and turned his head in the direction we'd originally come from. "I think I smell the bakery that way."

"Okay."

He shot me a look as we turned to walk into the village. "Are you well, Matsuko?"

"No. But I want food and I want to get out of here. We're not safe, Arach, and I don't like being not safe." I kept my strides purposeful even if I didn't know where we were going.

"What do you feel is going to happen?" He kept up with me without appearing to hurry.

"I don't know, but the longer we stay, the worse it gets." I tightened my lips and kept my eyes open. There was something wrong with this village but I couldn't see what it was.

"You could always cast a spell of illusion, making us either appear to be not here or just forgettable." He sounded so reasonable as if doing magic was an everyday occurrence.

"I told you I don't know how to control the magic. Do you believe I know any spells?"

"Spells, as I understand it, are really just words used to focus your intent. This is why 'abracadabra' is such a popular phrase among sorcerers and magicians. It's not the word, it's the intention behind it. You could use your favorite nursery rhyme while focusing on making us disappear and we would."

He led us to the bakery where the baker had set out a few of his wares on a set of rolling shelves beside the door. "Go ahead, Matsuko. Make us forgettable in the minds of the people here."

He left me standing outside next to the bakery cart as he ducked through the door and I blinked. He expected me to be able to do this. Why didn't I?

Because I've never learned how to do magic.

But only because my family and friends didn't believe it could be done. Was it really that easy? *Spells are really just words used to focus your intent.* Maybe I could make us forgettable with just a little spell.

I started to hum a well-known pop rock song and pictured what I wanted in my mind. The gist of my focus would allow us to walk through the town, interact with whom we needed, and then fade away from their awareness after we'd gone. Invisibility in memory.

The energy built up behind my sternum and migrated down to my hands. I pictured us fading from view, people's eyes skipping over us before their minds could interpret what they'd seen, and them having no memory of us if questioned later.

"The sun and the moon, the wind and the rain. Hand in hand, we'll walk on by, forgotten before the birds can fly. We'll have nothing to lose, we'll have nothing to win, we'll just escape this town and never come back again."

Blue light coalesced between my hands until I held a shimmering bubble of writhing strands. When I solidified the image in my mind, I tossed the ball of light up into the sky. It widened and grew, expanding to cover the whole village before it popped like a soap bubble and sprinkled a pixie dust-like substance over everything.

Arach returned a few moments later with a bulging

pack and a satisfied smile. “Ready?”

“So ready.”

“Good. The baker was rather chatty this morning and he said that it was a good thing we came in when we did before all those damn soldiers ‘His Lordship’ has gathered come in and raid the place for the local garrison.”

“Who’s His Lordship?”

Arach shook his head. “I didn’t find out, but he lives about ten miles up the road from here in a fortress they call Dark Reach Keep.”

“That sounds welcoming.”

He shot me a grin and laughed. “My glory, did you just make a sarcastic joke?”

I tilted my head to look at him from under the hood with one eye. “Did you think you had a monopoly on snark here?”

He laughed again. “No, my lady, but I’m delighted to share in yours.”

His laugher was infectious and I smiled as we made our way past the inn and out to the northern edges of the village. The commercial buildings and residences gave way to tilled fields and livestock grazing. The tension had released its grip on me the farther we traveled from the village, but I still kept a wary eye on the road.

We passed farmers working the fields but they didn’t even bother looking up at us. I couldn’t tell if it was because of my spell or because they’d been so downtrodden by the garrison soldiers. But the people in the village itself hadn’t seemed frightened or cowed.

Maybe my spell really did work.

The road had dried despite the water I could still smell in the air. The temperatures were mild and our path wasn’t too difficult. There weren’t many on the road, so we made good time. Then my stomach growled.

“Either you’re hungry or you’re keeping a baby dragon hidden somewhere beneath your dress.” Arach grinned at me as I rolled my eyes. "Let's see if we can find a dry place to sit for breakfast."

The fields had given way to swamps with tall, water-loving trees like alders and willows. Some had large enough roots protruding out of the soil to provide shelter from the wind, camouflage from the road, and a dry place to settle for a bit. Arach led me off the road and spread his coat on the root of a big willow.

I sat down, enjoying a moment of not moving and Arach's scent wafting up from his coat each time the breeze teased the willow branches. The scent reminded me of his body over mine and his penis in my vagina, and the pleasure in his voice and face when he was with me. The memories warmed my insides and made me smile.

We didn't talk much as we feasted on bread, butter, a little bit of dried meat he had found somewhere, and some spring carrots he'd swiped from the baker's counter when the man wasn't looking. Arach assured me they wouldn't be missed, but I wondered if someone's carrot cake would take longer to make than expected.

We'd packed up the remnants of our meal just as strident voices and footsteps filtered through the rattling of the willow's leaves. Arach shot me a look and placed his fingers over his lips in the universal gesture to remain quiet. I nodded and we peered through the branches to see what was going on.

A large troop of soldiers, each bristling with weapons and weighted down with thick leather armor marched toward the village. Most of them didn't look anywhere but ahead, but there were a few who kept their gazes roving over the landscape, acting as guards for the group. The tense feeling I'd had in the village returned and I shrank down as small as I could get behind the willow's fronds.

"Where do you think they're going?" I whispered the words, afraid I'd be overheard from the road.

Arach shook his head. "I'd bet they're going to the

village to look for some outsiders who came in last night." His expression grew uneasy. "We'll wait for them to get out of sight beyond the trees before we keep going."

I nodded. "Do you think their barracks are nearby?"

He shrugged, his gaze on the retreating soldiers. "They might be in the next village or farther on, but either way, I don't think we want to meet them on the road." He glanced back at me. "You might have been onto something about getting different clothes. It's best if we don't make it easy for anyone looking for us."

When the soldiers disappeared, I got ready to move, but Arach held up a hand. "Wait."

I frowned. "Why?"

"Just watch."

For a while, there was nothing to watch, and I wondered if he had lost his mind. But after about five minutes, two more soldiers trotted into view, one on either side of the road and dressed in much lighter armor with bowstrings stretched across their chests.

"Scouts," he whispered. "Looking for people hiding from them."

"Like us." I swallowed hard.

"Exactly."

Once the lightly-armored archers disappeared from sight, Arach agreed we should get moving. My heart thundered in my chest, and I worried they'd somehow double back and catch us, but most of the tension had left Arach's shoulders. However, his eyes kept roving across the view as if searching for anyone who seemed out of place.

No one disturbed us as we neared the next village, but we did catch sight of the garrison fort and barracks. It was an imposing place with high walls made of sharpened tree trunks and guard towers. It reminded me of a state prison, but the gates were open and I could see men practice-fighting in the courtyard beyond.

Fortunately, we weren't the only ones on the road. This was a much bigger village and had wealthier-looking homes and commercial buildings. When we entered the outskirts, we found a livestock market and a large central square with a dais in the middle of it. Some imposing houses stood around the square, but little pop-up stalls filled with goods showed this was the market day for this town.

"We should be able to find more than one inn here and get some new clothes if you're interested." Arach waved at the stalls. "But keep an eye on your belt pouch. In towns this size, there are bound to be pickpockets."

"Before we go shopping, can we find a place to stay for the night?" I shot a look over my shoulder the way we'd come. "I'd like to have somewhere we can hide, should the soldiers come back this direction."

"But your spell…"

"Will cover the people in the last village but won't cover the soldiers coming back here if they should find the people matching the descriptions they have."

He glanced around and pulled me closer to the space between two stalls. "Wouldn't it make more sense to change our appearances first?"

I rubbed my arms and kept my gaze moving. "Maybe, but are you sure someone won't steal our bag while we're trying on clothing? Wouldn't it be better to have a place to leave it?"

"Inns aren't always the most secure when you're not in your room." He too scanned the busy marketplace. "I think we should find what we need and then find a place to stay. We can change there and go out later if needs be." He pointed across the square. "I see a leather goods vendor. We can start looking there."

I followed him through the shoppers, keeping my eyes peeled for smaller people picking the pockets of the adults. There were quite a few nimble children zipping in and out of the crowd. I hadn't found a belt pouch in my things, but I couldn't remember if the guards had taken it off me when I arrived in this world. Too worried about where the hell I was to pay attention to what I had on me.

Turned out there were more shops beside the one selling leather. We bought waterproof hoods, belts with attached leather pouches, elegantly-tooled arm braces and matching vests, and a rucksack for me from the leather vendor. The next shop supplied warm woolen cloaks, trousers, and several pairs of socks. The third merchant sold linen shirts and chemises, along with a lovely, padded overcoat with brightly colored autumn leaves embroidered into the cuffs and hems. I admired the coat but decided I didn't need it, no matter how pretty.

Arach happily paid for everything and we stowed our purchases in our rucksacks.

"Where are you getting all this money to spend?" I followed him back into the square and deeper into the town.

"Some of it's from a dragon's hoard." He grinned as he avoided a fruit cart being pulled by a vendor. "And some of it's from some unlucky locals. I told you to keep an eye out for pickpockets." He winked and I couldn't help but laugh. Wily dragon.

CHAPTER EIGHT

Arach

For a moment I thought maybe Matsuko would reprimand me for pickpocketing the locals, but she laughed and I let out the breath I hadn't known I'd been holding. Not everyone approved of my skills, particularly not rule followers like my elder brothers and father. They did this big song and dance about honor and integrity, but they were the ones who often withheld from their allies their ability to shift into fearsome fire-breathing beasts. And they used guerrilla tactics when fighting. When I'd pointed out it was only honorable when it suited them, they hadn't been very happy with me.

But Matsuko had only laughed and followed me into the rabbit warren of streets and buildings, looking for a suitable inn. Nothing too ostentatious to stand out, but nothing too worn down to be a den of thieves. I'd spent many a night in places like that—I was a thief—and that was enough. We finally came across The Thorny Rose, which boasted actual side and back yards with trees and a garden to give the guests respite from the busy street. An attached livery stable let weary travelers store their mounts, and the clientele looked to be somewhere between the merchant class and the lower nobility.

I managed to negotiate for three nights at a decent price and paid with my own funds. Rule number four of thievery: Never steal from the patrons at one's place of residence. It was a good way to get dead sooner than one hoped.

Surprisingly, we were given a room with a view of the garden in the back. While I would've preferred a street view so we could see who was attending the inn, the trees were soothing and I relented when I saw Matsuko's expression.

"Those look like cherry trees. I bet they smell wonderful in the springtime when the flowers come out." Her voice sounded so wistful, I vowed to find her a cherry tree of her own when we finished the quest.

But she didn't stay at the window long. She stripped out of her dirty traveling clothes and pawed through the new items buck-ass naked. I was struck dumb watching her lithe body move, all that glorious golden skin reminding me of the moments I'd spent touching her. She changed into the trousers, linen shirt, vest and arm braces, and settled the belt around her trim hips. I just stood there and watched even when I was supposed to be changing, too. But she was too beguiling.

"I could definitely use a pocketknife or some sort of small blade." She paused and looked up at me. "Are you okay, Arach?"

"Uh, what?"

"Are you okay? You're just standing there. Don't you need to get dressed too?"

"Oh, yes, yes of course."

She'd finished her fashion ensemble with the cloak and leather hood by the time I'd pulled on my new trousers and shirt. Of course, the thoughts of her showing off her legs made my cock take notice and rearranging it took more time. I added the arm braces and my long vest and belted it to my hips as she laced up her new boots. I already had a knife, though with my claws it was for show only, and a set of lockpicks that worked much better than claws any day.

"I have a knife you could use, but it fits my hands better than yours." I pulled on my cloak and added my hood until we both looked like a couple of rangers. "When we go back to the market today, we'll look for something suitable for you."

She straightened and gave me a thorough examination. "You look like Robin Hood."

"Who?"

She grimaced. "Robin Hood. He was a legendary hero from my world. Stole from the rich, gave the loot to the poor, who'd been overtaxed to fund the rich overlord's lavish lifestyle."

I smirked. "Well, I am a thief, but it's usually funding my own lifestyle."

"But don't you have a hoard, since you're a dragon and all?" She folded her old clothing on small bedside table with a grimace. "We really need to wash this stuff." She wrinkled her nose. "Yours probably too."

"Are you suggesting I stink?" I raised an eyebrow.

"After days in the same clothes, some of those in prison? Yes." She shot me a dry look and I laughed.

"You make a good point. We can inquire of the innkeeper if there's a laundry service."

"Okay. Are you ready to go?" She straightened and she definitely looked like a ranger minus the bow and sword.

"I am. Let us see what kind of trouble we can get into." I grinned but she shook her head.

"No, let's see what kind of trouble we can avoid. Like Assassin's Credo."

I frowned. "Are you an assassin by trade, Matsuko?"

She shook her head as she led me out of the room. "No, I'm an audiologist, but I played computer games, and Assassin's Credo was one where you were an assassin, but your goal was to get the artifact you were looking for without anyone really noticing you. You might have to kill some people along the way, but that wasn't your goal."

"But assassins kill for money. That is their whole purpose. Someone pays them to eliminate a rival. There's no honor or credo, as you call it." I scowled. "Why would you play an assassin for fun?"

She took a breath to answer, but her expression turned pensive as I locked our room door behind us. I was a thief, not exactly the bastion of morals and honesty, but I made every effort not to kill anyone. The burden of someone's death wasn't something I could carry very easily and I didn't want it. It was beyond my understanding that someone would want to pretend to be an assassin for entertainment.

We took the stairs down to the common room and went straight through without speaking until we reached the street. The sun shone down on us but the dampness of the air made us grateful for our cloaks. I reminded myself we needed to get Matsuko a suitable knife for her to carry, but unease slithered along my spine. Would she prefer to be an assassin?

She was quiet a long time, following my lead as we returned to the marketplace. I kept my attention on the young pickpockets who wove in and out of the patrons while scanning for a smithy. We found the blacksmith working on a war ax, sharpening the curved blade as his foot pumped the pedal to make the sharpening stone turn. We watched him for a while and I wrestled with my mate's interest in a death dealer's lifestyle.

When he'd finished the ax, the blacksmith came to see what we wanted and nodded to our request. He presented us some knives and Matsuko looked them over carefully before picking up a few. She finally found one that had good balance and fit in her smaller hand. The blacksmith nodded approvingly and named a price. I didn't even haggle, just handed over the coin. The quality and workmanship was worth it.

"Are ye sure you doona need a sword, rangers? Ye canna get far in the Warmonger's army without one." The blacksmith shook his head.

Matsuko and I exchanged a look before I returned the blacksmith's frank gaze. "To be sure. But we're only recently arrived in Aldmarsh from the Redwynne Plains near the Holtwater Sea. Who is this Warmonger and why is he amassing an army?"

"Och, he's a johnny-come-lately general who needed somethin' to do and got folks all stirred up to go to war against the Aelmoors up north. Ye havenae heard?"

I shook my head.

"Aye. He's supposed to have a voice as sweet as honey and beguilin' as a bloody siren. Has the young men and women flockin' to him in droves to sign up for his war." The blacksmith scowled in disgust. "Waste of good people, if ye ask me. The Aelmoors never caused us no trouble."

I shared another look with Matsuko. This had to be Warmonger's use of the Song Stone.

"But I bet your business is doing well in preparation for this war of the general's."

"Aye, weel enow, but it's blood money, the lot of it." Disgust twisted his scowl deeper. "Bloody waste, it is."

"I believe you're right." Matsuko laid her had on the blacksmith's arm and I had to bite back a growl. "Perhaps you can tell us where Warmonger is located so we may avoid him or his troops?"

"Och, lassie, you canna avoid them. There's a barracks here in Rivertowne, and the big brutes wander the streets at night lookin' fer whores, drink, and trouble, and they doona seem too particular." The man wiped his hands on a rag before picking up one of his newly made blades and sliding across a whetstone. "But his main stronghold is up the road apiece, some three miles northeast of here, in the old

Sarkaeny Fortress they now call the Dark Reach Keep. Ye canna miss it, but I'd advise against makin' a visit unless yer enlistin'."

I stiffened at the name. I'd been to that fortress when I was a child. It had been the home of one of the aristocratic dragon families, my father's sister and brother-by-law. And now Warmonger had taken it over? Where were the dragons?

Matsuko nodded and smiled. "Thank you. We'll definitely take your advice. Thank you for the blade."

She drew me outside and pulled me toward the center of the square near the dais. No one was making pronouncements so most people there were sitting down to rest in the sunshine for a bit. She made sure we weren't near anyone when we stopped and then she stood in front of me, her eyes searching mine.

"What's wrong, Arach?" She studied my whole body but the tension wouldn't leave my shoulders. "Are you still mad at me about the computer game? I've been thinking about what you said, and you're right. No one should think being an assassin is great for entertainment. I think the draw is how mysterious they seem and at least in this game, the object is to get in and out of places without being discovered. You lose points for getting caught by the guards and for killing innocents. But you're right. There's no honor in killing for money. You're better off being a simple thief and only killing in self-defense."

"There's nothing simple about being a thief," I snapped, but it wasn't at her that I was angry. "But that's neither here nor there. We need to find the library or the archives."

"What? Why?" She tilted her head.

"Because I've been to the Sarkaeny Fortress when I was a boy. It was the home of the Sarkaen Dragon Family, my paternal aunt and uncle." I lowered my voice as I glanced around, noticing more guards in the market square. "If Warmonger has taken over the fortress, where are the dragons and how long have they been gone? We need to visit the archives."

"Do you think the archives will tell us what happened to the family?" She followed along with me as we headed back into the twisting streets of Rivertowne.

"They might, but I'm more interested if they have architectural plans to show how to get in and out of the fortress, where the secret passages are, and alternate entrances."

"Why would anyone make the plans to a fortress available in the public archives? Isn't that a good way to let your enemies in?"

I nodded, a sardonic smirk curling my lips. "Oh yes, a very good way. But when the designer is an arrogant cockalorum who wants kudos for his magnificent creation, he keeps a set of his own. And when he dies…"

"They're donated to the archives."

"Exactly."

I led her toward the inland side of Rivertowne, away from the market and the river wharves. The archives would need to be on drier ground where the mold and the wet wouldn't get to the paper collections. There was a possibility we had a way to get into Warmonger's fortress. All we needed was a plan.

****

Matsuko

Relief bounced through me at Arach's words. He'd accepted my apology, mostly, and brushed me off for his concern about his extended family. Who the hell could take on a family of dragons and displace them? I followed Arach through a different part of the town, heading away from the river toward the higher ground. The buildings became stately and governmental in their construction and if the people here had universities, this was where I'd expect to find it.

Instead, a structure rose out of the earth beyond the last governmental building, reminding me of some fancy offices that had been built near my house in my world. Sharp, crystalline spires jutted out into the air creating a jagged line against the sky. In my world they called it art deco or industrial chic, but it just looked sinister and forbidding ahead of us.

"This is the archives?" I shivered with unease. "Please tell me we're not going in there."

Arach tilted is head and inhaled deeply. "That's where the plans to the fortress will be. You still want to get into the fortress, yes?"

"No?" I gave him a hopeful look.

He chuckled. "Ah, I see. You'd rather avoid this daunting task even if it broke the rules, or at least your agreement to the goddess Tekhne."

"I'd rather avoid the task, period. But I gave my promise." I sighed and rubbed my hands on my thighs to warm my suddenly cold fingers. "I hope your charm will work on the archivist because this place gives me the creeps, and I'm not sure they're going to believe two rangers want to look through maps and tomes."

He muttered something like, "me too" as he pulled open the huge wooden door with iron hinges. Surprisingly, it made no sound despite its size and weight and we stepped into an interior filled with shelves of books and a polished marble floor. A long, intricately woven runner led from the door to the great wooden circulation desk where a Black man with a trimmed silver beard and round spectacles sat making notes in a large ledger.

"May I help you, rangers?" The man's voice was deep and soothing like the purr of a relaxed cat.

"We certainly hope so." Arach's voice turned friendly and charming without obsequiousness. "My partner is new to this part of Greylea, and I wanted to give her a sense of the land, structures, and geography of this area since I spent much of my time here as a boy. And I knew this was the finest archive outside of the Isle of Sageshore."

The archivist beamed. "This is very true. I thank you for the compliment."

Arach inclined his head with reverence. "However, I was surprised to learn that the Sarkaeny Fortress is no longer occupied by the Sarkaen Family. What has happened to the family? Did a plague befall them?"

The archivist shook his head. "No one seems to know and they haven't been by to update the records, which is unusual. The family were sticklers for accuracy and would always send a messenger to us here at the Archives to bring us the yearly events.

"But since General Warmonger and his rowdy band of hoodlums moved in, the family has not been seen or heard. It's most unusual." The man scowled and shook his head with a disdainful twist of his lips. "They're nothing more than brigands and thieves, looting and destroying precious artifacts and history."

"Have they looted the archives?" Arach actually sounded horrified.

"No, thank the gods, they've contented themselves with the spoils of the fortress, which were not inconsiderable, I might add." The archivist sniffed. "Trolls, the lot of them."

"I'm happy to hear the archives are untouched. We were hoping to get into the map room and look not only at the famous buildings in the local area, but also at the geography." Arach injected relief and hope into his voice and the archivist responded with a smile.

"Of course, of course. Rivertowne has some of the most renowned architects and artists Greylea has ever known." He slid off his stool and came to the side of the desk. "The maps and architectural designs are kept on the second floor to protect them from flooding should the river rise this far."

"Sound thinking." Arach winked at me as we climbed the stone steps to the second floor behind the archivist.

The man was spry for his apparent age and he bounded up the steps with enthusiasm. "The Sarkaen family helped establish Rivertowne and sank quite a bit of money into building up the town, including the building for the archives. This building has been here for over two hundred years and houses treasures and maps from the time when the elves lived in more places than just Kampos Isle."

He led us into a room with two large glass windows on either side of the door, and shelves lined the internal walls. The room was lit by hurricane lamps set at intervals of every two shelves in sconces that held them high enough to broadcast light but far enough away from the walls to keep from setting anything on fire. The outside of the building had given me the creeps, but this space was warm and welcoming, and I was happy to spend as much time here as I could.

"The drawers here are where we keep the maps and architectural plans. They can be rolled almost all the way out and the maps may be lain on the tables for clearer study. All I ask is you not take the maps out of the room and please replace them in the drawers from which you take them." He smiled as he let us past him to the shelves. "They're all in alphabetical order, according to location."

"Are the architectural plans labeled the same?" Arach waved at the drawers.

"They are stored by location and then in alphabetical order of architect's name."

"Brilliant. Thank you, Lord Archivist."

"I shall leave you to it, then. Again, please replace the maps where you find them."

"We will. Thank you again."

The archivist left us, closing the door softly behind him, and I raised an eyebrow at Arach.

"Do you think he suspects we're interested in more than

maps?"

Arach shrugged as he pulled out a drawer showing the maps of the region around Rivertowne. "I don't know. But let's spend some time looking over the maps first just in case we weren't convincing enough."

We studied the hand drawn map of the town and the surrounding lands. The river split in two a few miles north of Rivertowne and the town sat on the eastern bank of the eastern fork, named the Sunblood River. Marsh forest had been marked on the map on either side of the Sunblood, but the ground turned rocky in spots closer to the large tributary from Dragon Skull Lake on the border of Aldmarsh and Aelmoor. The tributary had been named Dragon Blood River and continued south to feed Greywell Lake.

According to the map, Sarkaeny Fortress sat on a rocky promontory above the spot where the Sunblood River broke off from the Dragon Blood River.

"It looks like the road continues north from Rivertowne and skirts the promontory where the fortress was built." I followed the line drawn on the map. "Given the contours, I'd say they'll see us coming unless we can either find a secret entrance or look like the rest of the soldiers moving in and out of the fortress."

"I'm pretty sure there's a secret entrance on the north side of the promontory."

I raised an eyebrow. "You're pretty sure? I thought you said you'd been there before."

"I have, but it was almost a century ago and I haven't thought about it in decades. Who knows what they chose to change since I've been gone?" He spun back to the archival drawers. "Let's find the plans for the fortress and see if we can puzzle out where they put things."

"You're sure they'll be here?" I helped him look for the names of things. "Do you think it would be under Rivertowne or Sarkaeny?"

"I'm sure. Not under Rivertowne. Look under Sarkaeny."

I found the name. "What was the architect's name and how do you know he had kept a set of the plans?"

"His name was Beauregard, Augustus Beauregard, and I overheard him confiding in his scribe, a lovely young woman whom I suspect he was tupping, that these plans were so good he wanted to make sure he kept a copy of his masterpiece at home. Ahh! Here they are."

He unrolled the vellum to show several drawings of the same footprint with different levels of walls, floors, and hallways marked on each layer. It reminded me of the old school animators at the cartoon studios in Hollywood. Each layer had to match the previous one to show how the characters would move when the layers were put together in a movie reel. It was the same thing here, except there was only blue ink and the different lines showing where they'd carved into the rock or built stone walls.

Arach paused and looked around, making sure no one passed outside of the map room. He was silent and watchful so long, nervousness crept up my spine and made me hold my breath in case I heard something.

After several heart-stopping minutes, he nodded and dropped his gaze to the drawings.

"Yes, I remember now. Look here." He pointed to the north side of the promontory. "There's a natural cave here that lets out above the marshes on this side. My cousin Calron once told me his paternal grandfather had dug it out all the way to the site of the fortress in case someone came calling and didn't take no for an answer. It was a way to escape if they were overwhelmed. We followed it one night after our parents had gone to bed. You know how dragonets are."

When I raised my eyebrows, he snorted. "All right, perhaps you don't know how dragonets are. But we followed the tunnel all the way from the wine and root cellar, here." He pointed to the underground floor of the fortress. "The exit is almost three miles distant. The gap between the rocks at the mouth is no more than the width of a horse, but it appears to be a dead end until you turn to the left. Then you can smell the fresh air and see the opening a few more feet ahead."

"If your cousin knew about it, don't you think he'd mention it to your aunt and uncle?"

Arach shook his head. "Not this cousin. He wasn't the favored son so he left as soon as he had his majority, taking as much of the hoard his father had squirreled away with him. It infuriated my aunt and uncle. But he's been long gone so even if Warmonger subdued the family, he wouldn't have known about Calron."

"That's good. I hope your extended family is okay, and Calron seems interesting." I smiled when Arach laughed. "But we won't be able to take these plans with us so we should find a way to copy the information we need to take it with us."

"What do you have in mind?"

"Archives are basically a library, and all libraries have bits of paper and pencils to make notes if you can't take the materials out of the building." I looked around the room, skipping over the shelves full of books and scrolls. I found a wooden podium with a box full of loose sheets of parchment and some graphite styluses wrapped in wax paper. "This should work. Give me the written directions of how to get where we're going and what we're looking for—landmarks, internal entrances, things like that—and we'll give ourselves a written map."

"That's ingenious." He gave me a look of approval as we set to work.

It didn't take us too long to make some crude drawings of the interior of the fortress with likely places to keep the Song Stone as well as alternate escape routes returning us back to the tunnel. I wrote down everything he told me and made him repeat it because even if we lost or destroyed the notes, writing helped me remember what he'd said. I constructed the map in my head while I drew it on paper.

I'd just finished the last inscription when we heard noise coming from somewhere in the archives. We shared a look.

"I'll get our notes."

"I'll return the plans."

We hastily gathered up our research, Arach returning the vellum sheets to their drawer while I rolled up our notes and took the extra parchment and graphite stylus back to the podium. Then I skittered back to the table where Arach leaned over the first map we'd pulled out. I couldn't fathom why I was nervous, but my gut told me we didn't want anyone to know what we'd really been studying.

I made it back to Arach's side, but I noticed the drawer for the architectural drawings lay gapped. I swallowed hard as he pointed out the way the forest surrounded the western edge of the marshes just before the door to the map room opened. We looked up in surprise as the archivist stepped through the doors, his expression tense.

"I apologize for interrupting your lessons, rangers, but something has come up and I need you to come back another time to finish." He carried an air of apology along with a firmness that said we wouldn't be able to convince him to change his mind.

"Of course, Master Archivist. We were just finishing up." Arach smiled as he grasped the map and returned it to the drawer.

I backed up as he passed and "lost my balance" to close the drawer with the fortress's plans. Arach noticed and raised his eyebrows.

"Are you all right?" Concern tightened his lips.

"Yes, just a bit lightheaded. I think I need some water and food."

Arach nodded sagely as he closed the map drawer. "We

have been here a while. I think it's time to find some supper before we continue on our way. Master Archivist."

We nodded to the older man as we left the room and he followed us, tension wafting off him like a perfume. I soon learned why as we descended the staircase to the ground floor. I damn near swallowed my tongue.

General Dorian Warmonger stood beside the circulation desk with a weaselly-looking scrawny white man wearing spectacles, and two of the large hulking soldiers we'd seen in the village the day before. I drew my hood up onto my head in preparation to step outside but grateful it would also disguise my features in case the general looked up. I caught Arach doing the same as we reached the ground floor.

Fortunately, only the skinny scholar and the guards paid us any attention as we headed to the outer door. The archivist returned to Dorian's side.

"The map room is now open and clear for your research, General."

I swallowed hard and stepped outside, hoping my footsteps were purposeful but unhurried. Arach and I didn't speak at all until we'd returned to the rabbit warren of streets and the company of people. By unspoken agreement we headed straight back to our inn, keeping our attention on who noticed us, who followed, and who attempted to pickpocket us. We made it back to the inn without mishap and I breathed a sigh of relief as we stepped through the doors.

The proprietor smiled at us as we passed the bar and asked if we would like some supper. Arach agreed and the older man who looked like he had some Indian heritage led us over to a relatively quiet table under an elegant brocade tapestry depicting women in saris dancing. He handed us warm towels to wash our hands as he took our order.

"Thank you for the towels. They're a welcome treat after our day." I didn't know where I found the courage to speak up, but the way our host smiled and his cheeks turned rosy made it worth the effort.

"You are very welcome, mistress ranger. We will have your supper out in a trice."

"Thank you. Would it be possible after supper to have some hot water in a pitcher and some more cloths sent up to our room?" I waved at the ones he held in his hand. "I would like to take a sponge bath."

"Of course, but if you prefer, we can bring in a tub." I could almost see the coins rattling in his eyes.

"No, that won't be necessary. Just a pitcher and cloths will be enough."

"Very well, mistress ranger. We will arrange it. Will there be anything else tonight?"

"Might we arrange for a laundry service?" Arach finished with his cloth and handed it back. "Some of our traveling clothes are stiff with sweat and dirt, and we need them cleaned."

"Of course, of course. I will send our girls up to collect your things once you've returned to your room. Eight coppers for the laundry and sponge bath, please."

Arach placed a piece of silver in his hand. "For your excellent service and discreet kindness."

The innkeeper bobbed his head in gratitude. "You are very welcome, master ranger. We shall endeavor to continue this."

After he bustled away to help other customers and presumably put in our supper orders, I shot Arach a surprised smile. "Either you're feeling extra generous or you were bribing him to keep his mouth shut."

Arach smirked. "A little of both. I've learned that a little extra scratch makes people a lot more willing to help and hide you when needed." He shot a look around the room to make sure no one was listening or watching us. "It might help a little later should the man we saw in the archives come looking."

"You mean…" I too looked around before lowering my voice. "Warmonger?"

He nodded and lightened his expression just as one of the serving women brought us some bread that looked like naan and a warm drink that smelled like Chai. We thanked her, to which she smiled and inclined her head, before ducking away to serve the increasing throng in the public room.

"What do you think he was doing there? I mean, I know he was looking at maps, but why did he pick today of all days?"

Arach shook his head. "Maybe he's getting ready to mount an offensive against the Aelmoors sooner than expected. The blacksmith mentioned an increase in weapons needed and recruits looking for a place in the army."

I nodded as I sipped my Chai. A little heavy on the cardamom, but still tasty. "It would make sense he was looking for maps to help him navigate the terrain between here and there. Plan where best to make a stand." I shook my head. "That's something I really never want to have to know. But it still seems a little coincidental that he was there when we were."

Our suppers arrived soon after that and we dug in, keeping our personal thoughts to ourselves. The clientele in this public room seemed more jovial and easy than the one in the village and I managed to relax a little. Still, I kept my eyes open for hulking soldiers and diminutive pickpockets. I looked forward to my bath and rereading my notes from the archives.

CHAPTER NINE

Arach

Matsuko's words stuck with me when we retired to our room and her pitcher of hot water and the clean cloths arrived soon after. Why *had* General Warmonger been there the same time we were looking at ways to get in to the fortress? It did seem too much of a coincidence and it bugged me enough that I didn't pay close attention to Matsuko when she bathed.

And that makes me a stupid fool.

By the time I was done thinking and worrying, she'd gotten dressed in her chemise and the serving woman had collected our dirty clothes for cleaning. Matsuko stood beside the little stove in our room, warming herself as she rebraided her long hair.

"Are you all right, Arach?" She glanced over at me as I sat down in one of the two chairs positioned on either side of the stove. "You became very quiet after supper."

"I was just thinking about what you said. It was coincidental that Warmonger showed up at the archives today. The thing is, I can't think of any way he could've found out who we were or what we were doing. Even if he'd gotten wind us from the village inn, we've changed our appearances and he couldn't be sure we'd come to Rivertowne."

She frowned and tapped her chin. "I'm sure plenty of people saw us leave the village and guessed where we'd end up by the direction we'd gone."

"Except you'd cast that spell to make us forgettable."

"Right, but we saw the soldiers after we left, which meant they were dispatched before I made the spell. For all anyone remembered, we could've gone south. And we have no idea if that group, platoon, squad, whatever, came back to the barracks here or kept searching." She shook her head as she pulled out the sheaf of notes we'd taken in the archives. "But logically, they'd expect us to come to Rivertowne because it's the biggest settlement and they'd have to return to their home barracks eventually. What doesn't make sense is his choice to come to the archives today, the day we left the village."

"The problem isn't what he's doing, the problem is we don't *know* what he's doing."

"And knowing is half the battle. G.I. Joe."

"What?" I blinked at her goofy smile. "What does that mean?"

She snickered and shook her head. "Nothing, just that the more we know, the better prepared we'll be." She waved at my rucksack. "Do you still have the book you swiped from the goddess's temple?"

"Book?" I blinked and she rolled her eyes at my feigned innocence. "What book are you talking about?"

Matsuko snorted. "Arach, you're a dragon, which means you hoard stuff. But you're also a thief, which means you're a kleptomaniac and more often than not, you take things that aren't yours."

"No, I only borrow them long-term." My voice sounded prim, even to me.

She laughed and shook her head. "Right. Borrow them

long-term. Okay, fine. I saw the book when we were in the village and you hadn't had it before then, so I'm pretty sure you got it from the temple. What is it? Something that might be useful in getting into that place? Or getting out?"

I rose and retrieved the book she'd mentioned. "I don't know, maybe. It's a history book, of sorts. On military tactics that humans often use against each other with references to when and where they were used. Seemed like an odd thing for a goddess to have in their temple, but since it was just sitting there with no one using it, I decided it useful to have a reference text."

"That might be really useful. Are there any mentions of this area or even the Sarkaeny Fortress in it?"

"Not in what I've read so far, but I'll look for them." I returned to my seat.

"Okay. I'm going to review our notes and see if I can picture both the map and the fortress well enough to know it when we see it."

I held up a finger. "Perhaps now would be a good time to set a spell on our room?"

She frowned. "Spell? What kind of spell?"

"Perhaps something to either dissuade listeners or make it impossible to hear anything coming out of this room."

Matsuko tapped her chin again and pleasure filled my chest at her willingness to embrace her abilities. She rose and bit her lip thoughtfully. My cock saluted her actions even while I wished I was the one biting her lips. She closed her eyes and took a deep breath. Then she began to sing as she waved her hands to gather up the light that appeared between them.

"In the distant night I saw, a thousand people maybe more. We were talking without speaking. They were no longer listening. And we had our time alone that no one ever shared. No one dared to break the sounds of silence." She tossed the ball of light into the air of our room and it exploded into shards of sparkling dust, settling everywhere before fading.

"There. That should do it." She returned to her chair.

I blinked. "That was beautiful, Matsuko. Did you make that music up on the fly?"

She grimaced and shook her head. "No. The music was written by someone else in my world, before I was born. But I used them as a template to give me a framework to focus."

"It was hauntingly beautiful. And quite effective, I suspect." I sat back in my chair. "I think tonight after you go to sleep, I'm going to take a flight over to the fortress. I'd like to see what they're doing within the walls. I also want to check if the cave entrance is where I think it is."

Her lips tightened. "I don't like the idea of you being anywhere near that fortress, but you're a dragon." She stopped as her eyes widened. "Do you think Warmonger knows that your extended family were dragons, too?"

I frowned. "No, I don't think so. If that was the case, the people around here would be talking about it, extolling his prowess of taking out a whole family of dragons. I think he got into their home by using the Song Stone and lulling them into doing his bidding."

"But that means he could use the stone against you, too." She let out a long sigh and scrubbed her face with her hands. "Okay, I can't think of this right now. I'm going to read our notes and get some sleep, and hope I have a better idea of what we're going to do tomorrow."

I nodded and settled back to read the historical tactics book. I managed to read a little of it but trying to concentrate with Matsuko in front of me proved to be more than my already whirling mind could take. My gaze kept sliding over to where she sat curled up in a fluffy chair, reading. In all my decades of living, I'd never met someone who researched and studied like she did. Hellwinds, even most of the wizards and witches I knew didn't do this much reading.

She said it calmed and helped her find her center when she researched, and I had to admit she did seem calmer after everything that had happened.

Being dragged to another world, learning she had powers, meeting a dragon and a goddess. Yeah, I could completely understand why she might be a bit out of sorts.

"Did I understand Tekhne correctly? Did they say they and Ignius both sponsored me to be here?" Her questions came out of nowhere.

I glanced up to meet Matsuko's gaze. "Yes, that's what they said."

She frowned, something she did a lot. "Why? Do they do everything together?"

I laughed as I set the book aside. "No, not at all. In fact, I'm surprised they did this together. I doubt they've forgiven Ignius for the loss of all the art and music when the Library of Sageshore burned the first time, and that was four hundred years ago."

A look of horror crossed her face. "He burned the library?"

I shook my head. "No, but some of his priests forgot to extinguish their sacred flames after a ceremony, and the wind drove them into the stables. All that straw and *whoosh!* Bye-bye scrolls."

"We had something like that happen in my world. The Library at Alexandria held so much ancient knowledge, but there was a fire and much of it was lost." She shrugged. "There are people who still mourn its loss now, though it's been over a millennium."

"I don't blame them. Libraries are important."

She sighed and rolled up our notes before stuffing them back into her rucksack. "I'm too tired to keep reading. I'm going to bed. The silence spell I made should work for as long as we have the room. The magic will only start degrading once we leave for longer than a full day and night if I did it right."

I set the book aside and rose as she climbed into the large bed and settled beside her, gathering her into my arms. She sighed in contentment as she lay with her back against my chest and all my worries flitted away into the background. Something about her touch calmed me as much as research calmed her. It was delicious and I dozed with her for a short time.

I woke sometime later with the lamps still burning and the fire in the stove down to coals. Matsuko had settled onto her side with her back to me, her breathing even. I slid out of the bed and padded over to the stove to add fuel before sealing it up for the night then headed to the door for my boots and the key to the room.

I stepped out into the darkened hall and shoved my feet into the boots, grimacing at their cold interiors.

I want to crawl back into bed with Matsuko.

But I had to make this flight to reconnoiter from above what had happened to my aunt's home.

I made my way down the stairs to the common room, thanking my lucky stars that they were well made enough to keep from squeaking under my weight. There was no one around—even the proprietor and his family had gone to bed. I suspected the front door was locked against the vagaries of night, but there'd be a door to the scullery open for the servants to come and go at unusual hours.

I crept through the darkened inn to the back entrance that let out to the garden we'd seen from our room. The night air was fresh and full of water, but only the wind rattled the leaves on the trees. If the space had been larger, I could've shifted into my true form there, but I needed more space and less curious eyes to make the change. I let myself out of the side gate to the street and took off at a jog toward the high ground near the archives.

There were a few moments when I had to stop and slide into the shadows between lanterns to keep the nightwatchmen from catching me. The locals weren't the problem. For some reason, there were squads of four soldiers from Warmonger's army wandering the streets. I recognized them by their armor and the insignia of a double-headed war ax on their tabards.

What in hellwinds are they doing here?

I kept going out of town but listened for any of their heavy footsteps. It didn't take me long to find the archives building, a strange shape against the night sky. Despite its oddness, I breathed a sigh of relief that I'd reached the outskirts of town. Forest stretched out behind the building that would give me the kind of cover I needed to keep out of people's awareness.

The scents of wet forest and dank dirt hit my nose as soon as I left the bulk of the buildings behind. The street lanterns and torches didn't reach where I walked into the gloom and gave me plenty of space to shift into my true form. I hoped someday Matsuko would be comfortable with my dragon self. Her first introduction to it was rather abrupt and unnerving.

I leapt into the air with a forceful downstroke and powered higher into the sky, angling toward the forest instead of the town. The last thing I needed was an overzealous guard thinking a dragon was coming to eat the inhabitants and shooting me full of arrows. My hide was tough enough to repel most of them, but I didn't want to chance anyone getting lucky.

Once I'd hit the altitude I wanted, I swung back through the night air toward the river. It was the easiest thing to follow to reach Sarkaeny Fortress. The crescent moon rose in the sky and provided just enough sparkle on the river to guide me the way I wanted to go.

The fortress wasn't hard to find, not when most of the guard towers around the curtain wall were lit up by torches. Hellwinds, there were even torches in the towers of the keep. I kept my distance so the light didn't bounce off my belly scales. The estate had a large greensward on the southeast portion and it was full of tents. From the scent rising off the ground, many bodies slept in them, almost exclusively male and unwashed. I snarled a little into the wind and circled back around.

What in the gods' names had happened to my aunt's family? Where were they and why were they allowing Warmonger and his throng of barbarian thugs to use their home as their base?

I took a few more sweeps over the estate before I turned on my wingtip to head back to the solitude of the forest beyond the archives. Given the size and number of tents in the greensward, I guessed Warmonger had about three thousand soldiers amassed at the fortress. I frowned as I retreated to the open area between the archives and the trees. Why would he need to attack the Aelmoors? Those people tended to be nomadic horsemen and cervid herders. They didn't have much use for treasures unless they'd recently discovered something of value.

Maybe they have another artifact from Anima's prison.

I stuffed my dragon self into my human disguise and shook myself until everything felt right—tight but normal. It always seemed like I wore a suit four sizes too small after shifting, but I preferred to live amongst humans and they had issues with dragons. I started my trek back to the inn as skittish as a mouse, which seemed completely incongruent given my true nature. But I didn't like what I'd seen at the fortress and agreed with Tekhne that we had to retrieve the artifact before Warmonger got his wish for battle.

I made it back to the inn without seeing any more soldiers, either local or Warmonger's, but a pall had fallen over the town as if even the buildings were holding their breath in frightened anticipation. It would irritate me to no end if Warmonger succeeded in getting his way and destroying Rivertowne and Sarkaeny Fortress. Overall, Greylea had been a peaceful place and I had no interest in changing that.

CHAPTER TEN

Matsuko

My internal clock made sure I was up at sunrise but somehow, Arach was up before me and he'd brought breakfast as well as the steaming Chai drink. I rubbed my eyes and staggered off to use the chamber pot. By the time I came back, I was hungry enough to eat all of my breakfast and half of his, which he graciously gave me with a suggestion that I'd need the energy.

"Why? What happened last night?"

Arach shot me a look of surprise. "Why do you think something happened last night?"

"Because I woke up and you were gone. I figured you'd gone out to scout around and see what's going on with Warmonger." I shrugged and kept eating.

He swallowed some of the Chai and nodded. "I did indeed. From what I could see, Warmonger has built an army of about three thousand men."

I blinked. "You could see three thousand men from the air, at night?"

He laughed. "No, but I can count tents and estimate from there. I suspect the rumors that he's thinking of striking against the Aelmoors is true and we don't have a lot of time. It's midsummer right now, and with autumn comes the rains and snows up in the Aelmoor region. I'd say we have no more than a few weeks before he moves the army north."

"Okay." I finished the food and nodded. "So, when do we infiltrate the keep?"

"Soon, but not yet. First, we must work on our skills and teamwork, and make a plan with contingencies." He gave me an unusually serious look. "This isn't going to be easy, and we'll want multiple ways out."

"Right. Okay. Where do we start?"

I shouldn't have asked. That launched what I thought of as Boot Camp for Novice Thieves. We started with avoidance exercises. These consisted of learning how to disappear in crowds, melting into shadows when someone was specifically looking for me, and appearing innocuous. We had to buy me more new clothes to blend in and be nondescript.

Arach was a patient teacher, but every now and again I'd catch his lips tightening in annoyance and I'd have to shove away the worry that he'd give up on me. He'd been doing these tricks for well over half a century. I was learning them now. He tried to teach me how to pick pockets, but I wasn't any good at it, and finally told him it was his job. He conceded the point and moved on.

Then he started teaching me fighting techniques, particularly hand-to-hand combat. I rarely disliked anything enough to feel strongly about it, but my emotional state when it came to those lessons made it difficult to concentrate. After yet another failed attempt to block his blow and disarm him, I started to hum as the anger overrode all my defenses. Flames licked along my arms and I had to breathe a few moments to settle them. That they calmed almost immediately was one small victory.

"Why do I have to learn how to fight? I'm a sorceress

here. Fighting is for soldiers." I stomped away from him to cool down and to catch my breath.

"I'm not teaching you how to fight, Matsuko. I'm teaching you how to deflect and avoid." Arach's voice held patient firmness. "I will defend you as much as possible, but I can't be everywhere at once. There's a possibility we could get separated, in which case you'll be on your own should you encounter any soldiers or guards."

"But I don't want to kill anyone. That's not who I am." I didn't think I could handle killing anyone on purpose. Not outside of a video game.

"I'm not teaching you to kill anyone. I'm teaching you how to be not-there."

"Not there?" I turned and frowned. "What does that mean?"

"I'm teaching you ways to deflect any of the blows thrown at you, in addition how to move to avoid them entirely. I don't want you to fight any more than you want to. My goal is to make you understand how to see where the blows will fall and not be there."

"Oh."

My anger and frustration cooled immediately, and I shifted my thoughts to learning his teachings. I mastered them quickly after that.

Most of our physical practice sessions happened outside of town in open meadows within the forest where no one could see us. When I asked what would happen if someone did see us, Arach assured me most people would believe we were rangers sparring to keep our skills up. It made sense to keep up the persona of the rangers and we caused no stir when it came to Warmongers soldiers or the local guards.

Learning defensive moves and avoidance exhausted me, so there were days we'd take breaks by hiking out to the forest behind the Sarkaeny Fortress to scout for the entrance of the tunnel. We tried to keep it low key, but there were times we encountered soldiers on the road coming to enlist or other people who wanted news of the area. Being rangers meant we carried news from one place to another while patrolling the forest. Arach slid into the role like he was born to it. He had grace and a silver tongue, and he always put the travelers at ease. It was impressive.

On the few days where we couldn't practice outdoors, we returned to the archives to view the maps of the towns to the north along the river just in case we'd have to find shelter somewhere other than Rivertowne. We were known in the larger town, so we'd either have to return south or find anonymity in the villages to the north and east. Neither of us thought we'd be able to cross the river to the west without him shifting.

We planned for several contingencies, practiced more defensive hand-to-hand moves, and hiked out to the forest every day for a solid two weeks. I ate more than I ever thought I could and fell into bed each night with deep exhaustion. I would've liked to have more sex with Arach, but I was too tired to do more than snuggle up to him. And he was always up before me in the morning with news of the reconnaissance flights he'd taken the night before.

This morning, after we thanked Mr. Yajna the innkeeper for his breakfast and his hospitality, Arach led me out to a new practice space. This had more rocks and dirt than vegetation and forest, and I raised my eyebrows at him as he settled himself in his teaching mode.

"Today, you're going to start mastering the art of offensive magic."

I blinked. "Are you trying to tell me I have to learn how to insult someone?"

He threw back his head and laughed. "No, although I think you'd master that as well as anything else I've taught you. No, I meant in terms of military strategies, like mounting an offensive against an opponent." He waved at a set of rocks ahead of us. “I want you to learn how to use your magic to deflect missiles, move obstacles or threats, and cause distractions to throw off our opponents. I suspect you’re going to need all three.”

It turned out causing distractions was the easiest of the three. Arach reminded me that my magic appeared to be tied to music, so I just needed spells I could memorize easily. Song lyrics became my templates, and I knew most by heart. I just had to modify them to fit our needs. For distraction, I used XTC’s “Mayor of Simpleton.”

“I’ve never been anywhere you’d think I’d be. Not even to a little degree. Some of your friends think that they’ve seen me, but it’s nothing that I’ll vouch. Well I don’t know what they think I could’ve done and they really need to get going home. And I’m not the one they’re looking for and they’ve already forgotten me.”

I put all my energy into making us less noticeable to passersby and used the Wallflowers’ “One Headlight” to offer true distraction.

“You see the sun coming up in the break of clouds, and the splinters of colors out loud. Look over there, a familiar face who’s vanished now without a trace, there’s no one here for you to place.”

Moving items, picking them up and throwing them somewhere else, proved to take more energy and practice. Inertia didn’t care if I had magic or not, so combatting its presence took concentration I didn’t know I possessed. But using my knowledge of music helped. For physically throwing things, I used Urge’s “It’s My Turn to Fly.”

“It’s your turn to fly, away into the night. Gone and not returning, I fling with all my might. It’s your turn to fly, kiss your ass goodbye.” All right, the lyrics weren’t the most mature, but then neither was the idea of flinging people away from me.

Finding some way to deflect things thrown at me took a lot more focus, and several days of practice. As a human, I reacted to things in the usual ways, ducking, running, and dodging. But I couldn't concentrate on making a spell if I had to hide my head or duck out of the way. It took nerves of steel and extraordinary focus. I finally turned to Kelly Clarkson's "Catching My Breath." It was an earworm, easily remembered, and quick to arrive when needed.

"Coming into another time, distance causing a mesh of life. Catching darts in a web of lines, I've sent them from my heart. Sending waves out to combat shadow missiles and baseball bats. Watching stones and this and that, I've sent them from my heart."

I'd finally mastered the deflection and the other spells came when called without much effort five days into our third week. While I'd been run ragged, I was enjoying myself and Arach's patient teaching routine. I even made him laugh a few times while practicing and I loved the sound. It became a better reward than his usual praise.

"All right, last lesson." Arach brushed off his hands and stood after our lunch.

I blinked as I scrambled to my feet. "Last lesson?"

He nodded. "For the purposes of our upcoming altercation with Warmonger, yes. This is more of an offensive move that will give you the reputation of a dragon's mate."

"I thought I already was a dragon's mate."

"Oh, you are."

He growled and pulled me close, tilting his head to kiss me deeply. I let myself get carried away with his erotic enthusiasm. Pleasure zipped through me and left me breathless.

"But now you'll be able to convince others you are." He moved to my side and pointed me in the direction of the unmoved rocks.

"Okay." I tried to focus, but his kiss had left me all discombobulated.

"Take a deep breath, Matsuko." Arach's voice sounded

calm and confident, but those tones only sent excitement through me.

No, not excitement. Something else. Something powerful and exciting and unusual and uncomfortable. I thought I had a handle on this world with its magic and strange creatures, but I still couldn't figure out my emotions with regards to Arach.

He's a dragon. Yes, a real dragon who could shift shape and fly and breathe fire. Which was why he was attempting to teach me how to control my own powers. Powers I'd gotten when Tekhne and Ignius had blessed me with their patronage.

I'm mated to a real dragon. My breath stopped.

"Are you breathing, or did you go back to that place where you overanalyze things?"

I blinked. "What?"

He chuckled. "That's what I thought. I need you to focus on the here and now. It starts with the fire in your center and channeling it into your hands." He moved to my back and took my forearms in his hands. "Do you feel the fire in your core?"

Oh, I felt the fire, all right, but it was more about his hands on mine and his body pressed against my back. And the memories of how he touched me. How had I forgotten how hard and warm and sexy he was?

"Deep breaths now and reach for that core of light and heat."

His voice was hypnotic as I tried to remember what it was like when the flames rose with my fear or anger. The feeling of roiling energy settled in my chest and tumbled over itself, building stronger and higher.

"Arach?" I swallowed hard as the energy rose from my belly, through my chest and shoulders, and down my arms.

"Yes, sheshtana?"

"I don't think I can hold it." It was getting harder and harder to dampen with each second.

His hands slid to my waist. "Don't hold it. Let it flow."

I swallowed hard and extended my hands, letting the fire go. Blue flames streaked from the ends of my hands and splashed against the rocks, instantly burning away any vegetation that dared grow on their surfaces.

I expected the release of the flames to hurt, but instead I felt the call of them, urging me to play with their glorious heat for a while longer. Unfortunately, I began to tire pretty quickly and had to release them, cutting off the flow of energy. I staggered against Arach, exhausted enough to sleep for days.

"Whoa."

"Whoa, indeed." He sounded amused as he cradled me against his chest. "But that's enough for today. The only drawback to using those flames is they will drain you if you don't use them sparingly. Because you're a dragon's mate rather than a dragon, those flames will come at your beck and call, but they can't be sustained for too long or they'll consume your energy."

"Good to know. Can we go back to the inn now?"

"Soon. I need you to concentrate. This is how we'll build up your stamina to sustain those flames for when you really need them."

He gave me some water and more food from our lunch, which I inhaled like I hadn't eaten in days instead of minutes. Then he worked with me to create a small ball of fire to be held in my palm. This turned out to be a lot like an LED versus an incandescent bulb. It took far less energy to produce the flaming ball the size of a grapefruit than pouring flames at a distant object. He had me practice it many times before we returned to the inn for supper and rest.

I spent the afternoon and evening reading our notes on how we'd get inside the Sarkaeny Fortress through the tunnel and where the Song Stone was likely to be hidden. I worked on calling up the little ball of fire for my own amusement before banishing back into the core of my being as I studied, marveling at how easy it was.

Must be because of my connection to Arach.

I resorbed the flames and set our notes aside. Arach had gone to order supper to be brought to our room while I settled in to study. I suspected he was also arranging for us to stay a couple more nights before we made our attempt on the fortress. Soon, we'd finish the quest, bring the Song Stone back to Tekhne's temple, and I'd be free to choose what I wanted to do next.

The question was, what *did* I want to do?

I sat back and let my gaze slide out the window to the gardens behind the inn. I'd never been asked the question of what I wanted. Because of my autism, someone always decided what was best for me, even in my career choices and skills I learned. Family had told me what I needed to do to overcome my neurodivergent ways of seeing the world.

But here, with Arach and even Tekhne, I'd been given all the choices, and I'd been learning new ways to cope with what other neurotypical people seemed to understand so easily. I'd learned that I didn't lack the ability to cope, I simply coped in ways outside their imaginings. And the beings around me believed that I could understand, even if I didn't find my way to understanding the way they did.

That said, what did it mean for my choice at the end of the quest? I could choose to go back to my world and my life, help clients understand their hearing and the changes they faced, and my family, who only understood me as the autistic person I was there. No magic based on music, no illogical rules to the world, no dragons or gods or divine quests.

Or I could stay in Greylea with Arach, practice my magical abilities, speak to gods and goddesses. I could be a new person without the expectations of my old world, and I could stay with Arach, who I'd bonded with. He said dragons mated for life, however long that was, and I liked that aspect. I didn't have to guess how he felt or if he'd lose interest.

It suddenly seemed like my old world had gone monochromatic, devoid of color and life and magic. Did I really want to go back there?

At least I'd asked Tekhne to give me all the choices when the time came, and I might not get any choice if we didn't get the Song Stone back or died while trying. That was always a possibility. But I had to decide what I wanted. Either I asked to be sent home or I asked for something while I stayed here.

I was still mulling over the questions when Arach returned with our supper carried by one of Mr. Yajna's daughters right behind him. They'd added a fruity yogurt drink at no extra charge because they were grateful for our generosity and ease as patrons. It was tasty and I let my heavy thoughts go to enjoy the meal with Arach.

That night when I crawled into bed beside him, I wrapped my body around his and hugged him close. "Don't go out tonight, Arach."

"What? Why not, sheshtana? We need to know how Warmonger's army has grown and how close they are to marching on Aelmoor."

"Not tonight. I just want you to hold me. Please, Arach?" I met his gaze and held it, not sure why it was so important that he stay with me, but my gut insisted. His decision would influence the one that I'd been wrestling with since before supper.

"All right, sheshtana. I'll stay in tonight with you. Let me get undressed."

An unusual sensation settled into my gut and I remembered feeling something similar when my grandmother had promised to make my favorite kind of sushi at home. Excitement, pleasure, and contentment all rolled up in joy. I watched him undress until he stood naked beside the bed and arousal added to the rest of the emotional stew.

"I'm going to bank the stove and turn down the lamps."

I was good with that. I watched him move around the room in the dim light and enjoyed his nakedness. I loved how his muscles flexed under his skin as he moved and the bounce of his penis on his testicles as he walked made my vagina squeeze tight. It felt empty and I wanted to change that.

When Arach crawled back into bed, I reached down between his legs and slid my fingers under his testicles, weighing them in my hand.

"Is there something you'd like, sheshtana?" He sounded amused in the darkness.

"Yes." The answer was simple. "I want to touch your penis and testicles until you get hard. Then I want to suck on them like I've seen in the porn videos at home and have you come down my throat."

He groaned and his penis started to harden in my palm. "All of that sounds divine. But I do have one question."

"Yes?" I kept rubbing the length of his shaft, enjoying the stiffness under the hot skin.

"What about your pleasure? I have recuperative powers, but not necessarily quick enough."

I shook my head. "Giving you this pleasure is pleasure for me. I've wanted to do this since you made love with me the first time. I've been too tired, but tonight I'm not." I moved over between his legs, and he widened them to make room. "Can you reach the lamp? I want to see what I'm doing."

He made a sound resembling surprise and twisted his body to light the lamp beside the bed. I'd been impressed with his flexibility while we trained and chalked it up to his dragon essence. Once the lamp flooded light over the bed and he resettled on his back, I pushed the blankets off enough to see his muscular body.

"I like the shapes of your muscles." I traced my fingers over his chest and down his midline between his abdominals. "They make me feel unsettled, but in a good way. And I like these shapes here."

I stroked the oblique muscles outlining his mound down to his groin where they flared into his scrotum. He moaned as my fingers traced the lines, sliding from the small, lacy-looking scale pattern into the larger, darker pattern to mark his groin. I liked the color change and it gave me more of that good unsettled emotion.

"Do you like my touches, Arach?"

"Yes."

His penis flexed in front of my nose and I had the overwhelming urge to catch it with my hand and lick the top. When I followed my internal directive, he hissed and clenched his fists in the bedsheets. The skin on the tip was hot, smooth, and slick from the natural lubrication seeping out of the slit in the head. I opened my mouth and wrapped my lips around the edge of the head, settling it against my tongue.

"Oh, sweet gods, Matsuko." His voice held a rough quality that showed his strain, but I couldn't tell if it was good or bad.

I pulled back and looked up his body. "Yes?"

"For all that's holy, don't stop."

"Okay."

Relief tripped through me as I put his penis back in my mouth. I liked it there, the taste and texture pleasant against my tongue. I stroked the taut flesh, finding all the different textures along the shaft and the edge of the head. Each one gave me something new to focus on and given the sounds he made as I touched them, he liked my focus.

In one hand, I held his penis and the other I used to trace the line of his obliques down to his scrotum. He was hairless, but the skin was soft and fragile. It gave me a sense of power, to control his pleasure or pain depending on how I touched him. He wasn't complaining as I rolled the soft sack of skin in my hand. It tightened up just as his cock grew harder in my mouth.

I squeezed my lips around him and sank down so he slid deeper into my mouth. He groaned and rocked his hips, which surprised me as I wasn't ready for him to move. But it gave me a chance to rise and fall on his shaft, swallowing around the bulbous end. I rubbed his testicles in my fingers and sucked harder on his penis, and suddenly he moved, pulling his penis out of my mouth and yanking me up his body.

"I need you, Matsuko."

I blinked. "Okay. I thought I was giving you pleasure."

"Oh, you were, but while I love feeling your lips around my cock, I much prefer to give and take pleasure together." He tugged my chemise over my head and tossed it aside. "Ride my cock, Matsuko. Let me look into your eyes as you bring yourself to pleasure using my shaft."

The words were somewhat cheesy, but when delivered with the burning intensity in his expression, my whole body flared with arousal and all my surprised disappointment from being interrupted melted away. I crawled over his body and straddled his hips with his straining erection pressed against my vulva.

"Oh yeah. I can feel your wet heat on my cock."

"I can feel your erection against my vagina and it feels..." I ran out of words that fit the sensations. "Good" wasn't strong enough. "Erotic" was too clinical. "Amazing" sounded too common, overused, and not specific enough. "Pleasurable" was too vague. I shivered with the sensations, the hunger, need, and desire making it hard to find coherent thought.

"What do you feel, Matsuko?" He rocked his hips, stroking his hard flesh against my softer skin.

"Need. Want. More." That was the best I could do as the sensations swamped my mind.

“I can give you that.”

He reached between our bodies as I raised my hips and positioned his erection upright so when I came down, it slid into my vagina all the way to his testicles. We both moaned as I came to rest on his hips. Sweet gods, he felt perfect inside me. I wiggled just a little and the sensations made my breath catch.

“I’m not going to last long, Matsuko. I’ll hold out as long as I can.” Arach’s eyes blazed as he pulled his penis out and slid back in slowly. “Ride me with that sweet pussy of yours and give yourself pleasure. I want to watch you come all over my cock.”

I’d never experienced words enticing me or making me more aroused, but Arach accomplished both in his statements mixed with his motions. The slick slide of his erection in and out of my body stole both my breath and the ability to do anything but feel.

It didn’t take long for me to reach the tight, desperate place where my arousal crested into a release so sweet that I couldn’t hold back. Arach was right there with me and he growled so deep, it only added to the pleasure and stupefying joy cascading through me. I collapsed on his chest and tried to catch my breath, the knot in his penis keeping me anchored to him and the pleasure we’d created together.

“Whatever happens in the coming days, I want you to know I love you, Matsuko.”

The words flowed over me as I recovered from the explosion of passion inside and I wasn’t sure I heard them in a dream state. What did they mean?

“Love” was a word that had so many meanings and I’d rarely considered them. When I was growing up, I’d once asked my grandmother what love was because the way I experienced emotions was so different from the rest of my family.

“Love is connection, Matsuko. It is honor, duty,

integrity, and sacrifice." My grandmother's voice had been full of soft sadness. "It is making space for someone else's needs and desires in your daily routine, while they make space for yours. It is understanding both the differences between people and the similarities. Love is connection, mentally, physically, and emotionally. You will understand in time when you find the one who makes you feel everything and yet offers you a calm place to rest when the thoughts become too much."

I raised my head to meet Arach's gaze and I realized he embodied everything my grandmother had said. He understood me and listened to me and made space in his day and routine for me. No one had ever done that before. He also made me feel all the strange emotions and sensations, but when I needed a calm place, he provided that, too.

"Arach?"

"Yes?"

"I love you, too."

A slow smile curled his lips. "Are you sure? You sound hesitant."

"Yes, very sure, and not because of the sex. But I like that, too." I reached out and brushed the sides of his face with my fingers. "You make space for my needs and desires in your routine, and you offer me a calm place to rest. And that makes me happy and comfortable and welcome. It feels good and I want more."

"More sex?" He raised his eyebrows.

I smiled. "Yes, more sex, more time, more love."

"I can do that."

The heat and delight in his voice wove through me and when his penis hardened again, we made love slowly and thoroughly until we both feel asleep in exhausted satisfaction.

CHAPTER ELEVEN

Arach

Morning came earlier than I expected, but despite the early hour, I felt more rested and content than I had in decades. I'd declared my love for Matsuko and she'd reciprocated in her frank and direct way. I hadn't left the bed as I'd planned to after that. There was no way I'd leave my mate after she asked me to hold her.

But morning brought the reminder of what we needed to do and neither of us wanted to wait too long. We wanted to finish the quest, even if it meant she returned to her own world. I consoled myself with having secured her love, but I had no idea if it would be enough to keep her in my world. The thought dampened some of my contentment as we packed up our belongings, including the cleaned clothes left in front of our door.

Matsuko dressed in her sorceress's gown and hooded overcoat, but I wore my ranger's uniform. It would provide more protection in case we encountered anyone who tried to stop us in a more violent fashion.

"Are you ready?" I slung my rucksack over my shoulders and opened the door to the hallway.

“Yes.” She paused to take one last look at the room. “This is a good place.”

“It is.” I watched her catalog the room and all the good memories we’d made there.

“We won’t be back here, will we?”

I shook my head. “I don’t know, but after today, Warmonger will be looking for us and this place won’t be safe.”

She nodded then strode out the door and I closed it behind us.

“Let’s leave the Yajnas a good tip for their service. They were kind to us.”

I agreed and we descended to the public room that Mr. Yajna was opening to bring in the fresh morning air. We spoke with him a few minutes, offered our gratitude for his hospitality, and told him we were checking out. He was sorry to see us leave and grateful for the little extra I gave him in farewell. He gave us his family’s blessings and said we were welcome back any time. Matsuko waved and we headed out toward the market.

We managed to get a few provisions we needed, traveling foods, restocking our medicinal supplies, and new water skins for when we left Aldmarsh. As much as this had been a pleasant town, I’d be happier when we returned to places both warmer and dryer. The wet and damp soaked into clothing and spirits, and I missed the sun of lands closer to my first home in Redwynne.

From the market we headed through Rivertowne and out the north gate, manned by only local guards. None of Warmonger’s hulking soldiers tarried around the gates and I suspected he’d be leaving his fortress soon. That was both good and bad. If he left, it would be much easier to get in and poke around. I would’ve liked to shift and make an early morning reconnaissance flight, but we hadn’t traveled out of sight of the north gate and someone would pass the word that a dragon had been seen. So I hustled Matsuko at a fast clip toward the bend in the road that hid us from the town.

"Arach, wait, why are we running?" I'd forgotten she wasn't as tall as I was and I'd outpaced her in my hurry to get beyond the guards' view.

"I want to take a flight and see where things stand with the army. We don't want them to leave before we get into the fortress."

"Why?" She sounded out of breath and I slowed my pace enough to let her catch up. "Wouldn't it be better if no one was home?"

"Yes, unless Warmonger takes the Song Stone with him."

She grimaced. "Oh, yeah, there is that."

She didn't say anything else as we jogged around the bend and paused to check for other travelers nearby. We waited a few minutes, hoping we'd have the road to ourselves long enough for me to shift and get aloft.

"All right. Give me fifteen minutes to check everything and we'll continue." I dropped my rucksack and took a few steps away from her.

"Wait, Arach." She held up a hand. "Why don't you drop me off close to the entrance of the tunnel and then take your flight? That will be faster than me hiking to get there after you figure out what's going on."

"But someone could see us." I shot a look at the partly cloudy sky, the sun breaking through in ethereal shafts.

"Not if you fly close to the tree line and carry me in your hands. If we're in such a rush, it would be more efficient." She picked up my rucksack and stared at me expectantly.

I laughed. "Very true. All right. Give me a moment."

I took a deep breath and tried to quell my nervousness. The last time she saw me shift shape she hadn't been calm or happy about it.

Welp, she's bound as a dragon's mate now. Best she

know what she's gotten into.

Breaking out of my human disguise always felt like a release of too tight clothing. I didn't realize how uncomfortable it was until I took it off and breathed a sigh of relief. I sometimes wondered why I stuffed myself back into the smaller form, but then I'd remember why I hid my true form and now I had another reason. Matsuko.

I shook myself to realign all the bits and pieces—spines, scales, wings, horns, and claws—into their proper configuration before I dared look at my mate. I found her watching me with rapt attention, that intense focus she had when studying a map or reading her notes.

"I didn't get a chance to really look at you before. You're very beautiful." She stared up at me with her head cocked in consideration and admiration. "I'm ready to fly when you are."

I rumbled a laugh as I held out one of my hands. She climbed on and dropped the two rucksacks in my palm as she wrapped her arms around my thumb. I wanted to nuzzle her and rub her scent on my face, but we had too much to do in too little time to take that intimacy. Instead, I leapt into the air and climbed into the sky just enough to catch one of the thermals rising from the ground.

Matsuko tightened her grip on my thumb, but she didn't scream or cower in my hands. Instead, she looked over the edge of my fingers to watch the ground fall away from us. I couldn't read her expression as I kept my attention on the road beneath us. The last thing we needed as for a traveler to see a dragon and report it.

It took no more than a few minutes to cover where I was reasonably sure the tunnel came out on the northeast side of the promontory where the Sarkaeny Fortress sat. The vegetation had changed since I was a youngster poking about with my cousin, but the rocks were the same and I landed gently on the slope above the road nearly a mile distant.

"Where is the entrance from here?" Matsuko hiked both rucksacks onto her shoulders and started up the hill toward the outcropping of rocks above.

I considered her question as I probed the rocks with my fingers. My talons found the opening before my eyes did and I cleared away some of the brush that had clogged the gap.

"Good. Okay. You go see what's going on in the fortress and I'll wait here for you. Be careful." She met my gaze and patted my muzzle. "I love you."

Her simple warning and declaration warmed me more than the fire I carried naturally in my belly and I waited until she'd disappeared behind the brush to launch myself into the sky once more.

This time I went up high to just below the few clouds making the ceiling. I wanted to appear like a bird to most of the humans on the ground. I'd still have a clear view of the comings and goings of the fortress without putting myself in danger of being shot with an arrow or crossbow bolt. While they weren't deadly, they were extremely annoying like a splinter or thorn.

Wheeling in the sky, I made my trajectory to take me in a gentle arch around the front of the promontory so I could see the grounds and the keep of the fortress. All appeared relatively quiet. The number of tents had grown over the last week, suggesting that Warmonger had gathered roughly five thousand men for his upcoming campaign. They weren't packing up to leave, so we'd have to deal with them when we got into the keep.

That could be both good and bad. It was good because if we looked innocuous enough, they'd never bat an eye and with new recruits coming in all the time, we wouldn't seem out of place. But there were a lot more people to avoid and we'd have to work on appearing as though we were supposed to be there.

I swung away from the fortress to the west as shouts

came from below. I glanced down at the men on the battlements who'd caught sight of me and raised a mild alarm. I wanted to laugh as they pointed, but I decided it best if they thought they'd scared me off. They were in the home of dragons so a visiting beast should be a common sight, but apparently not. I winged away up into the clouds to the west and circled back to the northeast out of their sight. It still troubled me that my extended family had allowed Warmonger inside, but perhaps we'd be able to help them once we acquired the Song Stone.

I came down out of the clouds but had to head out east to wait for some travelers to move on down the road toward Rivertowne. It was a frustrating delay, but it couldn't be helped. The fewer people who knew a dragon was about, the better. It seemed to take them forever to cross the marshes and disappear into the forest. By the time I got back to the tunnel entrance, I was famished. I shifted as quickly as possible and joined Matsuko out of the wind.

"Everything okay? It seemed to take you a long time." She looked up as I settled beside her.

"Damn travelers. They moved as fast as oxen stuck in the mud." I scowled as I grabbed a chunk of bread from our rations and tore into it. "It was irritating."

"I can understand that. What did you find out about the fortress?" She munched on some dried meat as she set out the water skins.

"Warmonger's army has grown to roughly five thousand strong, which is both good and bad." I explained my reasoning and she took the information in with the focused look that told me she analyzed it as fast as I told her.

"Where does the tunnel come out in the fortress again?"

"The wine and root cellar just below the kitchens."

She nodded as she stuffed her food back into the rucksack. "That could work. We could slip in as new servants. With all those soldiers, they'd definitely have to hire more people to take care of them and we wouldn't stand out so much. What if we meet a member of your family? Will they raise the alarm?"

I shook my head. "I don't know, but I don't think so. If they have no problem with Warmonger and his men, they'd have less problem with us." I hoped. I hadn't seen my aunt's family since I'd left my father's home, and he hadn't been terribly pleased with me. I just hope that disdain hadn't infected my aunt.

"Okay, so how long is this tunnel?" She rose to her feet and set her rucksack aside in a darkened corner.

"About three miles."

She nodded. "How are we going to see if there's debris or roots in the path?"

I rose and placed my rucksack beside hers. We'd leave them there until we came back this way. It was the only way we'd make it out alive and I had no intention of either of us getting killed.

"You'll follow me. I have the ability to see in the near darkness." I took her hand and kissed her knuckles. "I promise to lead you true."

She smiled but it faded into a grimace. "Near darkness? Is there something that lights the tunnel?"

"There is. Do you have everything you need on you?"

She nodded. "I have my utility belt and my knife."

"Good. Let's get this adventure started."

I took her hand and led her into the tunnel. When we'd gone around the corner, the small luminescent crystals known from this part of Greylea faintly illuminated the tunnel's path.

"Oh my goodness, they look like airplane aisle lighting."

I didn't understand her reference, but I was glad she could see the light. Not all humans could.

"You could always make a magelight."

"A magelight?" She frowned and thought for a

moment. “Like a little ball of light that follows along with me like a lantern?”

I laughed. “Yes, that’s exactly it. And it’s just a—”

“A spell. Right.” She nodded and took a breath to sing. “You gotta just hold the light and let it burn, for all our steps and every turn. Cause that’s how the fire works, burning in bright colors, leading us on and on, all the way until we’re done.”

She held her hand up and a small ball of soft, golden light filled her palm. Her expression lit up with pleasure. “I did it.”

“So you did. Let’s keep going. We have a long trek to make it the fortress.”

We made good time with Matsuko’s light. Even though I could see the light from the crystals, her magelight made everything easier. When we reached the end of the tunnel, the more regular stone wall could be seen at the end with a heavy door with iron hinges stretching nearly all the way across the width.

“How do we get through the door? I’ll bet it’s locked.”

“It better be. Anyone who doesn’t lock this door is an idiot.”

My aunt’s family hadn’t been stupid, but I had no idea how long they’d been away from their home or if Warmonger had killed them, and someone else might have unlocked the door. Or they’d forgotten it was there completely. Or they were dead and couldn’t tell anyone.

I swallowed back my anger at that prospect and pulled out my lockpicks. Hopefully, the locking mechanism wasn’t rusted shut and there was no one on the other side, or our adventure would get very exciting quick.

It took some convincing to get the lock to turn but eventually, with a loud, protesting screech, the bolt pulled back from the doorjamb. We both stopped and waited, listening for the alarm to be raised, and hoping no one had heard the sound.

"I don't think anyone heard it." Matsuko peered over my shoulder as if the door would show what was waiting on the other side.

I swallowed hard. "I believe that's true. Shall we try it?"

"Yes."

I took a deep breath and pushed on the door. It moved a scant few inches and stopped.

"I think there's something in front of the door." I shoved it a little and heard another groan.

"Sounds like something heavy, like crates." She lifted the magelight and we peered through the gap. "Can you see anything?"

"I think it is crates with bags of something on top." I glanced over my shoulder. "Do you think anyone will hear us if I shove it hard?"

"Do we have a choice?"

There was that. "Okay then. Here goes."

I braced my feet and shoved the door hard, straining as I pushed it open. The sound on the other side was horrendous and I prayed to Tekhne that no one would hear. When I got the space wide enough for us to slip through, we both froze and listened again. The seconds ticked by as we held our breath.

"Do you hear anything?" Matsuko pushed forward until she stood in the space behind the open door.

"No, nothing." I followed her inside and peeked around the stacked crates.

The room beyond stood empty and silent. I didn't think anyone had been in it for a while given the layer of dust on everything. Matsuko stepped past the crates and surveyed the room while I closed the door to the tunnel until it latched. I left the crates where they were to disguise both the door and that someone had used it.

"Looks like a storage room for forgotten items." She swiped her finger in the dust on the crates and wrinkled her nose.

"Let's go into the wine cellar but be careful. People probably go in there more often."

We crept into the next room lined with shelves and bottles of wine covered in cobwebs. There were footprints on the floor, but no one had left any lanterns or torches burning. Matsuko's magelight bobbed along above her shoulder and cast a golden hue over everything as I glanced around at the shelves.

"Seems emptier than I remember." Only half the shelves held bottles. *Someone's been drinking a lot more wine lately.*

"Looks like there's a set of stairs up to a door. Does that lead to the kitchen?" She pointed past the shelves holding potatoes, carrots, bags of other stored items like apples and nuts.

"Yes. It should be pretty busy in there so be ready to extinguish your magelight and look like a servant." I led the way up the short staircase and grasped the door handle. "Ready?"

She nodded and snapped her fingers. The little magelight zipped to her hand and disappeared into her palm. Her mastery over her powers had become impressive. Taking a deep breath, I pulled the door open.

As I'd expected, the room on the other side was full of people working on feeding the five thousand other people outside the keep. Cooks shouted orders to the kitchen staff and no one looked in their direction. I didn't wait for someone to decide they needed something from the cellar and ducked into the room, Matsuko following on my heels as she tugged the door closed behind her.

The scents of stew and bread hit my nose and I tried not to gag. This wasn't the best food, it was only plentiful and hearty. I suspected Warmonger didn't waste the good stuff on his infantry. *Cannon fodder, the lot of them.* He just wanted them fed and ready to fight.

We skirted around whirling kitchen staff, trying to stay out of the way, but we didn't make it to the kitchen doors unnoticed.

"Oy! What are you doin' here, then?"

I pivoted, keeping Matsuko behind me until I met the gaze of a woman with reddish-gold hair and emerald green eyes. She wore a servant's uniform but he carried herself with the bearing of an aristocrat. It took me a few moments to see beyond her disguise.

"Deandra?" I took a step closer to her. "Is that you?"

She blinked a moment as her expression froze then she frowned. "Arach?"

"Yes." I moved closer but out of reach. I remembered how fast she was with the little blade she always kept on her.

"What are you doing here?" She narrowed her eyes. "And why are you dressed as a ranger? Are you working for Warmonger now?"

I shook my head. "No, definitely not. Can we go somewhere a little less busy to talk?"

She seemed to remember where we all stood and glanced around. "Yes, of course. Follow me."

I ushered Matsuko ahead of me as we followed my cousin Deandra Ironbones out of the kitchen and down a hallway to an empty room that looked like a child's parlor. Old wooden toys lay packed in crates and boxes at the edges of the room while the faded murals depicting animals and rainbows looked on. A thick layer of dust lay over everything and floated in the sporadic sunbeams that came through the uncovered windows.

Deandra rounded on us and narrowed her eyes. "Now, tell me what in hellwinds you're doing here, Arach, and who is your companion?"

"I could ask you the same sorts of questions, Deandra. Where is Aunt Shar and Uncle Dennith? What happened to the family and why in hellwinds have you let that mudfucker Warmonger in here?"

"We didn't *let* anyone do anything!" Rage suffused her normally serene features as she threw her hands out. "He showed up and Father let him inside. I happened to be out tending the gardens and overseeing the servants when he arrived. Because I stayed out of the way, whatever spell he's woven over my parents and brothers never got to me. He doesn't know who I am and I want to keep it that way until I can figure out how to get rid of him."

"What happened to them? Are they dead?"

Deandra shook her head. "No, but they have this sleeping sickness. They are more agreeable to anything Warmonger says and they can't be bothered to protest. And they sleep almost all the time, too drowsy to do much of anything. I don't know what's wrong with them."

"I'll bet it's the Song Stone." Matsuko's soft voice intruded.

"The what? And who are you?" Deandra was cutting no slack.

"Deandra, this is my mate, the Sorceress Matsuko Ishikawa. Matsuko, my cousin, Deandra Ironbones, of the Ironbones Clan."

Deandra's eyes narrowed. "Wait just a moment. Did you say 'mate'?"

CHAPTER TWELVE

Matsuko

When Deandra's gaze landed on me, I had the distinct impression she didn't approve of Arach's choice. I didn't hum this time, but I let the music fill my inner ear just in case I needed to call up some sort of shield to protect myself.

"How could you have gotten a mate and not told us?" Her emerald gaze swung back to Arach as she slammed her hands to her hips.

He chuckled. "Deandra, I haven't spoken to anyone in the family for over thirty years. No one seemed very interested in what I got up to, much less who I mated with. If it makes you feel better, you're the first one I've told."

The white woman with small breasts and wide hips under her housekeeper's outfit raised her golden eyebrows. "Not even your parents know about your mate?"

Arach shook his head. "No, you're the first. But that's not what's most important right now. I think I know why your family is so lethargic."

"Really? Gone for thirty years and you have the answers to everything?"

Tension strung Arach's shoulders tight but he gave a lazy smile. "When Warmonger arrived, did he claim a particular room for his own?"

Deandra tightened her lips and her eyes flashed fire. "He took Mother's solarium, claiming he needed the light to clarify his thoughts and strategies."

"That's different." Arach shook his head with an amused smile. "Can you take us to the solarium? I think he's gotten a'hold of a magical artifact that lulls people into amiability and if left unchecked too long, makes them sleepy and lethargic."

Those were jumps in logic since we'd never seen what the Song Stone could do, but given Deandra's description and Tekhne's story on what the stone had been used for, it made sense.

"An artifact?" Her eyes sparkled with what looked like greed. "What kind of artifact?"

I shot a nervous look at Arach. Would we have to fight his cousin to get the Song Stone back to Tekhne's temple?

"We haven't actually seen it, just a description. It's supposed to be a large stone that looks like a polished sapphire." I tried to sound matter-of-fact about it. Something about Deandra's interest made me uncomfortable.

"And you think this is what's causing my family's lethargy?" She turned her attention back to Arach.

"Yes." He didn't elaborate but tilted his head. "Why didn't it affect you?"

She shrugged. "I don't know. As I said, I was outside in the gardens. That suggests it needs to be invoked in some way. I decided it would be wiser to act as the housekeeper than be ensnared in the same spell that has my family."

"If we can find this stone and take it out of here, the spell will be broken and your family will be free." I met Deandra's gaze frankly. "And you can do what you like with Warmonger."

“My parents and brother will have much to say, I assure you. Come.” She headed to the door of the room. “I’ll take you to Mother’s solarium. Warmonger is usually out with his army at this time of day and when he’s in, it’s to eat luncheon in the dining room.”

We followed her out as she strode with determined strides down the hallway. The corridor opened up to a huge, wide space that served as a grand entryway with several staircases rising to the second floor. The vaulted ceiling had the night sky painted between the arches and great columns held up both the ceiling and bracketed the stairs. We crossed the polished flagstone floor and ascended the staircase across from the hallway from the kitchen to the second floor.

This had a series of scallops that allowed for people to stand above and look down on anyone entering the keep. I would’ve liked to walk around the entire entryway loft, but we were on a mission and I reminded myself it wasn’t a good idea to irritate dragons.

Another hallway led along what I suspected was the front of the keep and we passed several doors that opened to either side. Only the set of double doors with glass panes in them let light into the hallway and illuminated the parquet floor and the rich burgundy hall runner. Deandra opened the double doors and stood to the side to allow us into the room before closing them behind her.

I understood why her mother would like to be in this room. Huge floor-to-ceiling windows marched down the outer wall, letting the light in to reflect on the art and furniture placed around the room. A piano stood in front of the last window with two loveseats and a chair positioned around it for the listeners’ ease. A fireplace with marble inlay braced between two more huge windows, and the last window stood beside an ornate wooden desk with papers and baubles decorating the top.

“Warmonger spends quite a lot of time here. I always

find him at the desk, writing or reading." Deandra scowled. "It will take a decade to clean his filth from this place when he's gone.

Arach and I turned to the desk. I went straight to the shelves behind it, inspecting the little baubles and knickknacks stored there while Arach searched the desk. Neither of us expected Warmonger to store the Song Stone out in the open where anyone could see it, but he likely had it nearby or easily accessible. I tried to ignore a buzzing that filled the room as I poked through the items on the shelves.

Please, gods and goddesses, say it's not in his personal bedroom.

The buzzing grew stronger as I approached a gilt chest the size of a shoe box. Like a little motor, the whole chest vibrated as I touched it and I gritted my teeth against the hum. I lifted the lid of the chest and peered inside.

The same stone I'd seen in Tekhne's vision rested in a bed of black satin and hummed with a deep bass note that reverberated in my breastbone and ear canals. I wanted to rub my ears, but I couldn't trust Deandra not to swipe it out from under me while I tried to recover. Instead, I reached in and pulled the stone out, holding it my hands as I hummed the counterpoint to the sound frequency.

The silence was deafening.

"I found it." I turned around and found Arach smiling while Deandra scowled. "Let's get it out of here."

"Wait, you're taking it? It's in the Ironbones house. It belongs to us." She strode toward me to take the stone, but I used some of Arach's training and dodge out of her way.

"No, it doesn't belong to you or the Ironbones Clan. This belongs to the goddess Tekhne and it's to them we will return it." I wrapped the stone into one of my long sleeves and held it close to my body. "Your home is free and you're welcome to do what you like to General Warmonger and his army. But the stone is leaving with us."

The smile she gave me was neither friendly nor warm. "Oh, my dear sweet summer child, I don't think you understand. You won't be leaving until that stone is in my possession."

She advanced on me but stopped short as Arach stepped between us. "Deandra, you must let us go. This isn't meant to stay here. It belongs to the goddess."

"I must do no such thing. That's a powerful treasure and it belongs to us." She tried to move around Arach but hissed as he blocked her once more. It wouldn't end well or quietly if she got her hands on the stone.

The Song Stone.

I started to hum as I laid my hand on the warm surface of the artifact. The hum within the stone matched mine and I began to sing an old lullaby from my world.

"Let it go, and say goodbye, sleepy lady, you want to.

The work is done and all right, and there's nothing more to do.

Sleep well for now and wake all refreshed.

You shall forget we were here and that is for the best."

Deandra's expression grew slack and all the tension left her body. Arach blinked then shot a surprised look at me.

"What did you do?"

"Remember what Tekhne told us the Song Stone was used to do?" I removed my hand from the stone. "It's to lull people into compliance with whoever holds it." I shrugged. "I made a spell with it. She'll forget we were here and wake up refreshed as soon as we've gone. Besides, she'll have too much work to focus on getting Warmonger out of here. So let's put her somewhere safe and get the flock outta here."

"What flock?" Arach frowned.

"Never mind. Let's go."

"Right. Yes, good plan." He took Deandra's elbow and steered her toward the door to the solarium.

"Where are you taking me?" Her words were slurred

with sleep.

"Where would you like to go?" He raised his eyebrows at me as we hustled her out into the hallway.

"The summer parlor. There are so many pretty things in there. Good couches too."

I snorted but nodded. "Where is the summer parlor?"

"First floor, on the south side of the house, of course." Deandra rolled her eyes.

"Of course." Arach patted her hand. "You just show us where and we'll get you there."

With Deandra directing us, we made it along the hall to the second floor loft and down the staircase. I kept my gaze moving around just in case we encountered any soldiers or servants who questioned who we were. We made it across the entry flagstone floor and into the hallway the led back to the kitchens. But she had us open the solid oak door and escort her into the opulent room on the other side. There were plenty of fainting couches as she'd mentioned and she settled onto one of them with a grateful sigh.

"Deandra, will you be well?" Arach stood back as I inched toward the door.

"Perfect…" She closed her eyes and breathed deeply before totally relaxing into the cushions.

"Damn, that thing is powerful. Let's get it and us out of here." He strode to the door and opened it, letting me out first before following.

And we came face to face with General Dorian Warmonger.

Oh shit.

I ducked my head and side-stepped so I had somewhere to retreat should he move on me. My heart rate ratcheted up with my anxiety and I had to think of something to keep the flames from rising on my arms. *Waterfalls, rain on my grandmother's pond, hot tea with Arach.* The last image made my heart swell and calm filtered through my whirling thoughts. Warmonger didn't know us, even if he'd seen us in the library, and he couldn't know all the servants in the keep. We'd be fine. I hoped.

"Who, in the name of all that's unholy, are you?" The blond man with fierce gray eyes and a blade for a nose looked down it at us though Arach stood a good six inches taller.

But Arach bowed with just the right amount of humility and adopted an air of diffidence.

"Ranger Sven, m'lord."

"What are you doing here? Who sent you? Who's she?"

"This is Druid Ishikawa, m'lord. We were patrolling the nearby lands and wished to make our presence known to the Ironbones family. We are caring for the forests and animals therein."

"Didn't I see you at the archives a few weeks ago?"

"That's very likely, m'lord. I was there to research some of the local maps with my partner."

Though I kept my head down under my hood, I could tell Warmonger had shifted his gaze to me. "The family is indisposed at this time."

Arach nodded. "So we have just learned from the housekeeper. We've just left her. She's given us leave to restore some of our provisions from the kitchen before we depart."

Again, Warmonger seemed to be looking at me. "Does she say anything?"

"No, m'lord."

Warmonger froze. "No? Is something wrong with her?" He backed off a few paces along with his guards.

"She only speaks to the plants and animals of the forests to determine what ails them." Arach shrugged. "And even then, she only sings."

"Sings." It was a statement rather than a question.

"Yes, m'lord."

"Why are you patrolling these lands?" His abrupt change in subject momentarily caught Arach off guard.

“They are forests, m’lord. And it’s what rangers do.” I could hear the ‘duh’ in his voice but his expression remained honestly surprised.

“What makes you think these forests need rangers? We’ve had no problems here.”

I wanted to argue that he was the biggest problem in this place, but that would expose us to unwanted attention. Besides, Arach had said I didn’t speak.

Maybe he’d send us on our way if I started singing “It’s a Small World After All.”

“We just wanted to make the family aware of our presence. We haven’t encountered problems, m’lord.” Arach sounded so agreeable that I wanted to check if he was all right. “As I said, the housekeeper will pass on our message to the family and we’ll just replenish our supplies before we’re on our way.”

I wished Warmonger would let us go as I didn’t want him to get to know us better than he had and I hummed under my breath. Power flickered in my chest but it didn’t extend beyond my body. At least, I didn’t think it did until Warmonger waved us toward the kitchens.

“Very well. Be on your way and get your supplies. But do not return.”

“Yes, m’lord. Thank you, m’lord.”

I thought Arach laid the obsequiousness on a little thick, but Warmonger and his guards let us continue down to the kitchens without another word. I breathed a sigh of relief that he’d let us go, but the kitchens were no longer the safe haven we expected. Two massive guards stood near the door to the cellar scrounging for their own snacks.

“What are we going to do?” I shot a look around the kitchen. Even the servants and staff were avoiding the soldiers.

“We’re going to replenish our provisions like we told the general and wait to see where the soldiers go.” Arach nodded to a kitchen child, a girl of about ten, and gave her a winning smile. "Good afternoon. The general instructed us to replenish our provisions for our journey. Would you be able to help us?"

The girl tilted her head to look at Arach and narrowed her eyes. "Do ye work for the general?"

"Not directly. My companion and I travel through the forests making sure the trees and animals are healthy."

The girl shifted her gaze to me and took in my sorceress's robes. I tried to be unthreatening and serene like my grandmother had taught me, and I hoped my nervousness didn't show. I held one of the most powerful magical artifacts this world knew and the guards could easily take it from me.

My grandmother's voice intruded with a sharp rebuke. *Child, no one can take anything from you if you don't wish to give it. If you project confidence in having what you have and being where you are, people will see what they want to see.*

I straightened my shoulders and willed the muscles in my face to relax. I was supposed to be in that kitchen getting provisions. There was nowhere else I was meant to be at the moment.

"Do ye really take care of the animals?" She directed her question at me and I nodded.

At least one big, scaly animal.

"Does ye speak aloud?"

I shook my head, remembering Arach's assertion to the general just in time.

"No, she only sings."

The girl frowned. "Why only sings?"

Arach gave her a secret smile. "Because music is universal and the trees and animals understand it best."

Her eyes widened and she nodded. "Aye, I understand that." She turned her attention back to me. "I wanna learn to speak to the trees and animals someday."

I nodded and reached for her hand to squeeze it,

shifting my gaze to Arach. I widened my eyes and tilted my head at the girl.

"All you need do is find a Druid to help you learn these things when you are ready." Arach's voice held gentle encouragement and I was tempted to go look for a Druid, myself. "But for now, perhaps you'd be willing to help this Druid and I find our provisions so we can be on our way?"

"Aye, I can do that." The girl smiled shyly at me and shook my hand with excitement before she released it and led us to a small pantry a few feet from the cellar door. "Here is the larder." She screwed up her face into a thoughtful frown. "We doona have much fruit because *they* took it all." She shot her gaze toward the soldiers who stuffed their faces with bread and cheese. "But we have lots of cheese, dried meat, and carrots." She stuck her tongue out.

"You don't like carrots?" Arach's amusement came through his question.

The girl wrinkled her nose. "No. They taste like dirt."

I grinned. *She hasn't had my mother's nutmeg carrots or carrot cake.*

"We'll take some of those, then." Arach chuckled as he snagged a nearby canvas bag.

The girl helped him pack for our "journey" as I kept an eye on the soldiers. They took their time eating and ogling the women in the kitchen, making lewd comments to anyone within earshot. It made me wonder when that behavior had become acceptable. It was the same in my world. No one spoke up when men were gross to others and I was sorry the same behaviors were seen here.

Eventually, the soldiers finished their snack and worked their way out of the kitchen, grabbing the women by their butts as they passed. Some shrugged it off, some squealed with coquettish amusement, and others skittered out of the way. None of the men in the room said anything. I turned my attention back to Arach and the girl.

“That’s excellent. I think we have enough meat and cheese. The carrots are in the root cellar, right?”

Oh, very smooth, Arach.

The girl nodded. “Aye, right over—”

“Eribella! Get yer arse over here and clean this silver!”

Eribella glowered and sighed. “Through that door. Down the steps and on this hand,”—she waved her left hand—“side. There’ll be bins.”

“Thank you, Eribella.” He gave her a short bow and she smiled with pleasure.

“Eribella! Now, ye silly gel!”

The harsh words only dimmed her smile a little as she scampered off to her next task. Arach lost his smile as he met my gaze and nodded. We’d been given our out and we were out of time. I suddenly remembered I hadn’t replaced the chest on the shelf behind the desk in the solarium and if Warmonger went there, he’d see it for sure.

“We need to go now.” I made sure my voice didn’t carry.

“Right, after you.” He yanked the door open and ushered me through before closing it behind us. “What’s the rush?”

“I forgot to put the chest back.”

“Chest? Which chest?”

“The one that held the Song Stone.” I hurried my steps through the wine cellar as I made sure the stone was still wrapped in my sleeve. “He’s bound to see it the moment he goes into the solarium. We don’t have much time before he raises the alarm.”

“Hellwinds.”

I repeated my magelight spell and the little golden ball popped out of my hand to drift up toward my shoulder as we hurried into the storage room to the stacked crates. Only our footprints marred the dust and I paused as Arach slipped behind the crates to the door.

“What are you waiting for? Come on!”

"We can't leave them all the clues." I closed my eyes and hummed a little nursery rhyme I'd learned in kindergarten. "Hickory dickory dock, the mice aren't liable to talk. They're off to race and left no trace, and the guards will have to take stock."

I stepped behind the crates and pushed Arach through the door as a little mini dust devil rose in the room, swirling the dust and cobwebs all over everything. I pulled the door shut tight as the magelight bobbed over my shoulder.

"There. Now we can go."

Arach led the way at a jog. "What did you do?"

"I resettled the dust everywhere and hopefully disguised our footprints. I don't want them finding the door very quickly."

He chuckled. "That's very smart."

"Thanks." I just hoped it would be enough to get us out safely.

CHAPTER THIRTEEN

Arach

I had to admit I hadn't thought about the footprints in the dust when we made our escape, but Matsuko's quick thinking had given us a head start on anything Warmonger sent after us. The discovery of the chest worried me. I hadn't thought of replacing it on the shelf because of Deandra's avarice, and usually that was something I'd do first.

Back when I was a real thief.

But I'd been more concerned about protecting Matsuko and getting out without Warmonger knowing we were there. *Carelessness like that is when mistakes happen.* Yes, but there was no help for it now.

I jogged steadily down the tunnel, grateful there weren't any turns in it until the end. My eyesight worked well enough to see the floor and Matsuko had her magelight to keep her footing. We kept going until we reached about two thirds of the way along the tunnel's length when I deemed us far enough ahead to take a bit of a rest. We weren't home free, but we'd made a good start and could afford to catch our breaths.

"We'll take a few moments to rest." I leaned against the wall of the tunnel and bent forward, feeling the adrenaline pumping through my chest with my blood.

But Matsuko shook her head. "No, we need to keep going. They're going to sound the alarm soon and we still have to run the rest of the tunnel. What if they figure out where it opens up?"

"Are you sure you don't need to rest?" I asked just as voices sounded at the far end of the tunnel. A set of torches appeared and someone yelled about a tunnel. "Hellwinds and damnation. Guess you were right. Let's go."

We took off again, this time jogging faster than before. The voices carried to us down the tunnel along with their footsteps. Our only saving graces were our lack of armor and the head start. We could move faster simply because we were smaller.

The next half hour was fraught with alternating panic and excitement. Matsuko didn't make any sounds beyond her breathing, but I imagined the guards behind us with crossbows. It made me want to tell her to extinguish her magelight, but there was no place to hide in the tunnel and she needed the light to see in the complete darkness.

"Keep going, we're almost there." My words huffed out in harsh whispers as we kept running. *We have to be almost there.*

A few more steps and the appearance of the dead end came into sight. *Oh, thank the gods!* I skidded to a stop and let Matsuko pass me. She ducked to the left with an expert move and I followed, trying to ignore the footsteps and grunts from the men behind us.

She'd already made it to our rucksacks and she deftly unrolled her sleeve and let the Song Stone drop into her bag before she buckled the straps closed again and lifted it to her shoulders. I reached for mine, but she batted my hands away.

"No. I'll take it. You need to get out there and shift.

They're coming and we don't have time to fool around." She pushed me ahead of her around the second bend as picked up my rucksack. "Go, Arach. Hurry. We need to get airborne in case they have crossbows or arrows."

I couldn't argue with that and ducked around the corner of the cave wall. She followed more slowly, the bags weighing her down. I wanted to help—I had that much gentleman in me—but she gave me a fierce look and a scowl.

Right, not the time for chivalry.

I burst out of the cave and shifted on the fly. It was neither the easiest nor the most fun way to attain my natural form, but desperate times made for faster efforts. I leapt into a dive down the hill, allowing my essence to come forward faster than I'd ever done before. Fortunately, my true self was ready and I literally dove into a dragon in a single bound.

Of course, that carried me well away from the cave entrance and Matsuko, leaving her exposed to the blackguards pounding down the tunnel. A spike of fear drove through my chest and I wheeled around, leaping back toward the entrance where she stood. Except she wasn't standing. She was crouched in front of the entrance with her hands over her ears and her face scrunched up in pain.

What the ever-loving hell?

I landed beside her and despite our need for escape, I shifted back into my human form, another quick shift that actually hurt to stuff the dragon self away. I ignored the pain and grabbed her shoulders. She didn't look up and panic filled my chest.

"Matsuko. Matsuko, what's wrong?"

She didn't answer and I resisted the urge to shake her. We had to get away and we were running out of time, but I couldn't speak to her in my dragon form.

Tears slid down her face as she whined and shook her head, her hands clasped over her ears. I couldn't do anything until she looked at me and unease snaked through me. What if she never looked at me? What if the guards caught up to us?

Sweet goddess Tekhne, help us both.

****

Matsuko

"I should not have come here."

I whimpered as the excruciating sound thundered in my head. It had come out of nowhere once Arach had leapt into the air and shifted into his beautiful scaly self. I'd wanted to watch him take flight, but the sound had blasted me and I'd dropped to my knees. I covered my ears and closed my eyes, but the sound was *inside* my skull and I couldn't get away from it. I sank to my knees and bowed my head. *Lady Tekhne, Revered Ignius, help me.*

I don't know why I prayed to them. They weren't my personal gods, at least not from home. But after having met Tekhne, I figured I had a clearer connection to them than the god folks from home claimed to know.

Someone grabbed me by the shoulders and shook me gently until I opened my eyes, tears running down my face. Arach. Why was he in his human form? He was saying something to me, but I couldn't hear him over the screaming noise in my head.

Aie, why are you so difficult? Read his lips. My grandmother's voice dripping with irritation pushed the screaming aside so I could focus. Whenever my autism overwhelmed everything, she'd remind me to read lips to find out what I needed to know, especially when everyone chose to ignore me.

"Matsuko, listen to me."

Heh, like that would happen. I blinked and nodded despite the sound.

"What's wrong? Talk to me, Matsuko."

"So much sound and noise. In my head. Won't stop."

His lips tightened and he shot a look over my shoulder. "I don't hear anything. You'll have to break it with your magic."

I shook my head. "Can't. Screaming. Can't focus. Don't know how."

He grasped my hands over my ears. "Your magic is your own, wielded in your own way. Bend it to your will. It will break the discord. Hum, Matsuko. Hum your favorite song."

My favorite song? I couldn't think of one. I had a veritable library of music in my memories, but nothing came to mind. Until maniacal laughter pushed through the screaming. And Ozzy Osbourne's "Crazy Train" filled my head.

The famous electric guitar rift pushed the screaming aside and I was able to enjoy the sound as the shrieking receded. I wiped my face as I kept humming the opening chords and he nodded.

"Good. Don't forget you have the Song Stone. It's under your power now. I'm going to shift, and we can be on our way."

He pulled back from me as I picked up the bags and shoved my hand into one of them. I touched the smooth warm sides of the stone. Immediately, the shrieking died away and Ozzy's music surged into the gap. The words of a spell rose into my mind and I projected them as Arach shifted.

"Coming here for me? Think you have the range? I'm going seal the cave with my wicked flames!"

Blue fire leapt from my arms just as Arach's taloned hand closed around me. The other hand plucked up the second rucksack just as he sprang into the air. We were just in time as the first guard squeezed through the gap. Caught in my spell, he burned to a crisp right in front of me, screaming in pain.

Oh, sweet glory! It shocked me into silence as he fought to get the flames off, but they consumed him too fast. Horror surged through me at the idea that I'd killed someone. It didn't matter that they would've killed me without a thought. I wasn't that kind of person. My flames died and other men shoved the burning soldier out of the way to take aim at us with their crossbows.

I squeaked as the fear overwhelmed me and folded myself down on Arach's fingers. But instead of blue flames, reddish-gold fire erupted above me, driving the men back into the shelter of the tunnel entrance. Dragon fire heated the stone around them and the quartz veins throughout the granite melted into liquid silica. The cries of the men faded behind the crystalline wall building from the molten silica until they were sealed behind a thick sheet of glass.

I gaped at the change in the hillside as the trees around turned black from the heat, but Arach wasn't waiting to inspect his work. He shot higher into the air with a powerful downstroke of his wings and the inertia shoved me into his palm. It took me a moment to realize he planned on hightailing it toward the goddess temple back to the south and I thumped his main knuckle to get his attention.

He tilted his head to look at me with one amber eye.

"Fly over the keep. Go back that way." I pointed toward the Sarkaeny Fortress. "We have to undo the spell Warmonger wove on your family to release them."

He growled something under his breath but wheeled in the sky and headed back toward the fortress.

"It's okay to be high up where their weapons can't touch us. The magic will work anyway. Just be sure to circle the whole keep."

He gained altitude while I shoved my hand back against the Song Stone and focused on the spell I wanted to cast. It would sprinkle down on everyone and everything in the fortress like pixie dust, working its way through the cracks in the stone and windows to dismantle Warmonger's spell. It seemed appropriate to use "Wish Upon a Star" as the template for the spell.

"Now I wish upon this star, quieting its voice near and far. Breaking its spell here once and for all as one must do."

Blue pixie dust trailed out behind us like a broken bag of glitter, sparkling in the pale light of the partly cloudy day. Arach started out low as he circled the entire Sarkaeny Fortress estate and rose ever higher, allowing the blue glitter to settle on every person and every surface. As he finished his spiral and winged away, the fortress and grounds shimmered in blue like one of those laser stickers I'd collected as a child. When the sun came out behind the clouds, the view was dazzling for just a few moments until the blue energy seeped into the stones and disappeared.

We flew over Rivertowne and the village where we'd stayed our first night away from the temple. I'd miss Rivertowne and its market, and Mr. Yajna the innkeeper, but I wouldn't miss Sarkaeny Fortress or the village. They could fall into the dusty bits of my memory without a qualm on my part. I could still see the soldier burning from my flames and it made my stomach sick. I was a sorceress and musical magic was my tool, but I didn't want to kill anyone ever again. I'd do my utmost to avoid that in the future.

The question was, what kind of future did I want? The goddess Tekhne had agreed to offer me whatever I chose and we'd be seeing them soon. So I took the time of our flight across the land to firm up in my mind what I wanted and what I'd ask for. I just hoped Arach would be okay with what I chose.

CHAPTER FOURTEEN

Arach

I wasn't sure exactly how far from Aldmarsh we'd come when the goddess Tekhne had sent us away, but I remembered it was up in the grassy hills above the Ribbon Rivers, northwest of the Redwynne Plains. So I followed the Dragon Blood River south to where it split again and took the east fork as the sun neared the western horizon.

Despite the lateness of the day and the adventure we'd had in the morning, I didn't feel tired at all. I had my mate with me, we'd vanquished an enemy, and I was able to spend more than a couple of hours in my true form. Definitely multiple wins, for certain.

The only thing that worried me was what Matsuko would choose when we faced the goddess again. Tekhne had promised to grant whatever Matsuko would ask for when it was time, but I worried she'd ask to go home. I'd seen her horrified face when she lit the first soldier out of the tunnel on fire, and I hoped it wouldn't make her choose to go home to the world that made sense to her. Her loss would be like a blade to my heart, but the decision was hers to make. I could only hope our connection over the past several weeks would balance out her fears.

Those thoughts occupied my mind as we winged our way south. The skies cleared and the moon came out, painting the river silver below us. I loved flying at night. Not only did it keep me safer from those who liked to shoot at dragons, but the whole world quieted down and things that weren't visible during the hustle and bustle of human occupation came out to be enjoyed. I watched a herd of Fright Mares, unicorns with savage looking horns and red eyes, flow over the hilly landscape out of reach of would-be hunters. Sleigh-Deer, the huge red cervids that could pull the winter traveling sleds of the nomadic Raimy peoples, dotted the river plain and my stomach growled. Just one would feed me for two weeks, thanks to my dragon metabolism.

I wished I could show them to Matsuko, but she'd fallen asleep in my hand, and I was loath to wake her. She'd performed admirably under pressure and helped us not only get what we sought but escape, too. She must have been exhausted. I pulled my hand up close to my chest and kept her warm as the night temperatures dropped beyond comfort at our altitude.

We arrived at the temple in the grassy hills just as the sun crested the eastern horizon. I landed closer to the structure this time and laid Matsuko gently in the grass before I shifted back into my human form. I stretched a little as I settled into my man shape and knelt beside her, brushing her face with the back of my hand.

"Good morning, sheshtana. We're here."

She opened her eyes and sat up, rubbing her face with her hands. "Here? Where is 'here'?"

"The temple in the hills where we met Tekhne."

I watched her stretch and yawn, her robes pulling against her full chest and I was reminded of our last night in Rivertowne when she rode me to completion. My cock stirred with the memory, but I told it to be quiet.

"Oh, wow, okay." She let her gaze slide around the landscape until it lit on the temple. "I guess it's time to return the Song Stone to Tekhne."

I nodded and tried to ignore the worry in my gut. At least it killed my cockstand. I helped her climb to her feet and watched her settle her rucksack on her shoulders. I picked up mine and did the same, but it didn't quite quell my nervousness.

"Are you okay?" She met my gaze with frank interest.

"I am." I tried to smile but it must have come out as a grimace because she frowned.

"What's wrong? Are you hurt?"

Not yet, I'm not.

"No." I didn't want to elaborate, so we continued the rest of the way to the temple in silence.

But Matsuko stopped me at the doorway and stood in my way. "What is wrong, Arach? Your body language is telling me you're unhappy."

I sighed. Not only could she read me from the outside, no doubt she could read my inner turmoil too. "We've come to the end of our quest, Matsuko. And that means you might be preparing to leave. And if I'm being honest, which is unusual at the best of times, I don't want you to return to your world. I want you to stay here with me."

"Oh, I see. Yes." She nodded but frustratingly didn't give me anything more than that as she entered the double doors.

I swallowed hard and followed her. What more could I do? The decision was all hers, but at least she knew how I felt about her. After all we'd shared, I couldn't imagine going back to my rootless lifestyle before I met her. I hadn't had this much excitement in half a century, and while not all of it was fun, it had been an adventure that I'd remember for all of my days left.

I wanted more time with her, time to learn her quirks and hopes and dreams. And I wanted to do it without familial interference. No doubt the story would get out of the Sorceress of Song and Flame and her faithful dragon bringing down one of Greylea's worst tyrants, and then my family would come calling to bask in whatever fame was granted both of us. But fame was more annoying than most suspected and anonymity had far more benefits. I didn't want our bonded relationship destroyed by attention seekers and glory hounds.

My family, in particular, would try to ride the coattails of my exploits. Prestige by association. I scowled.

We approached the central dais with the bench and I took a knee, still reverent despite my usual sacrilegious ways. This time, Matsuko bowed at the waist beside me, her hands placed palms together. Energy rippled through the temple like it had the first time we'd visited and soon, Tekhne reclined on their bench, the long-necked lute leaning against their thigh.

"Welcome back, Matsuko and Arach. It is good to see you both have survived your adventures." Tekhne nodded and smiled, the glowing white eyes gazing fondly at us. "Have you completed your quest?"

"We have, Lady Tekhne." Matsuko withdrew the glowing Song Stone from her rucksack and held it in her hands. "We have brought you the artifact you sought. Does our deal still stand?"

Tekhne inclined their head. "It does."

"Good. Okay, here's what I want." She raised her gaze to meet the goddess's. "I want a comfortable home near the coast of the Wandalup Bay, not too big, but not too small, and in a place where it's safe for a dragon to come and go in his natural form. And I want this house near a village, within easy walking distance, and a temple dedicated to you, as you're one of my patron saints."

I blinked. She was making conditions that would protect me. No one had ever done that before. Not even my blood-related family.

"I believe there is a temple dedicated to me in Dalup on the Wanda Peninsula. It's coastal but relatively remote so a dragon wouldn't be out of place." Tekhne inclined their head. "What else?"

I raised my eyebrows. The goddess was feeling very generous.

"I want enough funds, in whatever currency makes sense, to live comfortably. That is, not scraping by every day and every year, for the rest of my life. Think of it as my own hoard that befits a dragon's mate."

Tekhne grinned. "I think that can be arranged. But what would a sorceress need a hoard for?"

Matsuko tilted her head and smiled. "Life, the universe, and everything."

Tekhne snorted. "Very well, keep your little secrets, but your wish is granted. Anything else?"

"Just two more things. I want it to be known that I'm available to teach the local people about music and non-verbal communication. Spread a rumor or word-of-mouth advertising so that people find me when they need me."

"That's one thing, I do believe. What's the second?"

Matsuko took a deep breath. "I would like to speak to you directly, from time to time, at your temple. I want to retain this connection so I can learn more about this world and its rules. Then I can teach others about you and encourage their connection and belief in you and the arts you preside over."

I'd never seen a goddess taken aback before. For a few moments, Tekhne remained silent, their eyebrows up and one hand pressed against their chest in surprise. The goddess waited to see what else Matsuko would say, but after having traveled with her for weeks, I recognized when she had said all she needed and meant every word.

"You want to teach the next generation of humans about me?"

Matsuko nodded. "But only the good parts. You can

teach them your 'wrath of the goddess' on your own time. And you have to help Anima. I brought you the Song Stone. If she's awake, use it to calm her down and help her understand what's wrong. You said she is your sister. I bet she'll have an idea of what's wrong if you just talk to her and work through her ailment with her. She knows herself better than you know her, so she might have some insight. That's been my experience with my clients."

The goddess cocked their head and tapped their lips with one hand while stroking the lute with two others. I was a dragon and I had six limbs when in my natural form, but keeping track of all those arms would've exhausted me.

"You're wiser than you know, Matsuko Ishikawa. I grant all your requests as you asked them, with no hidden tricks or contract riders. And I'd be happy to speak with you when you visit my temple near Dalup. You've been a worthy paladin and you'll be a gifted speaker for me should the people wish to learn about me."

"Thank you, Lady Tekhne." Matsuko bowed again with her hands pressed palms together. "I'm honored with your gifts and gracious attention."

"Very well." The goddess rose and their gaze landed on me. "And because of your faithful service to my paladin, Arach Uzekamanzi, I shall grant your wishes as well. The Sorceress of Song and Flame and her dragon companion will become a legend, one your family cannot cash in on, and only a select few will know it was you and Matsuko. Now, it is time for you to go." The goddess waved their hands, all of them, and I braced for a shift in geographical space. "May the Music flow and buoy your soul." They clapped two of their hands and the temple disappeared.

We found ourselves outside a large cottage with thatched roof and a wide front garden. From what I could hear and smell, the cottage had to be near the shoreline of Wandalup Bay, and the cry of seabirds added to my assessment. Our rucksacks had come with us as we gazed at the home in front of us.

"Do you think this is what the goddess promised when I asked for a house?" Matsuko gestured at the front that had flower boxes attached to the windows and a red front door.

I shrugged and glanced down at the weight in my hand. A set of iron keys on a ring rested in my palm and I lifted them to show my mate. "These look like they might fit the lock on the front door. Not that we needed them to get in. Do you want to try?"

She nodded and pushed open the gate in the low stone wall containing the garden. Flagstones led the way to the door and I easily fit one of the keys into the lock. However, it didn't turn. Frowning, I had to try three more keys until we found the right one and I swear I heard laughter in the wind.

Never say a goddess told you things will always be easy.

The interior was both elegant and comfortable. The foyer had two benches on either side of the door for visitors to sit to remove their shoes. Matsuko immediately removed hers and hung up her overcoat on the hooks before continuing through the wooden archway into the house. Rugs covered the creamy marble floor of the sitting room furnished with a fireplace in dark gray slate, couches and armchairs with deep read cushions and colorful accent pillows, and end tables made from polished cherry wood carved with geometric patterns.

Matsuko nodded with approval and pushed deeper into the cottage to find a solarium with more of the creamy white marble, gauzy white curtains, and sliding windows to be open to the ocean breezes from the beach about a hundred yards from the house. I stood transfixed while she explored every room in the house, but if I'd been asked to pick a home most suited to me and my mate, this would've been it.

"There's no food in the house. We'll have to go to the

market."

"What, sorry?"

"We need provisions for our home." Matsuko smiled faintly. "This town of Dalup has fresh fish, don't you think? I bet we could make sushi if I can find the right rice and pressed seaweed."

I frowned. "You eat seaweed?"

"It's a special kind of seaweed called nori, but yes. Come. Let's go explore the town."

We put our boots and coats back on and locked up the cottage before heading into town. Matsuko found a hand wagon and dragged it along behind us. For groceries, she said. Like Rivertowne, Dalup had wharves and a market square with a central fountain, and a few inns and cafés. But the tallest buildings were only two stories and they were spread apart with wide streets and alleys twice the normal width.

We wandered the market, gathering up fruit, vegetables, poultry, some fresh specialty fish wrapped in wax paper, eggs, milk, a special kind of rice, and bread. She also found the seaweed she'd been talking about. I dragged the wagon as it filled up and found myself content in ways I'd never been. I also kept my eyes out for any easy marks in terms of pickpocketing, and the local pickpockets themselves. Dalup felt like home.

We got separated, but I kept Matsuko in sight while I sat at the fountain in the warm, sunny day with a small meal I'd procured in mostly honest ways, enjoying watching the people around me. No one was trying to kill or rob me, an unusual calm moment in a life of constant awareness. After a while, Matsuko returned to where I sat with one of her rare, secret smiles.

"I got something for you."

I glanced up from the meal as she held out a package wrapped in brown butcher paper and tied artfully with twine. A small glass crystal flashed in the sunlight near the knot in the twine.

"What's this?" I took the package, no bigger than a pastry box, and turned it over.

She shrugged. "It's for you. Open it."

I still hesitated. There was an old wives' tale among my people that said if someone gave a dragon a gift of the heart, the dragon would be bound to that person for all of their lives. I'd scoffed at the idea, but the old superstitions held strong in the back of my mind.

"Come on, open it. I promise it won't bite."

I snorted and untied the twine, carefully setting the box in my lap as I tore the paper free. What would Matsuko offer me that I couldn't simply steal?

The answer became very clear as I pulled the egg-shaped object out of a nest of packing grass. The orb fluctuated with the dance of the flower in the center.

"A fire flower." I breathed the words in awe before raising my gaze to her. "Where did you get such a treasure?"

"Do you like it?" She beamed. "There's a vendor here who does some really amazing glass art and his daughter is hard-of-hearing. I taught them some things in Sign Language so they could communicate better. Do you really like it?"

The superstitions are right. "I…do. It's extraordinary."

She frowned, tilting her head as she did when she heard more than I wished to say. "What's wrong? Did I cross an invisible taboo line?"

"No…" I shook my head decisively. "No, it's wonderful. I will treasure it always."

"Arach, please don't placate me. I won't learn if you don't tell me what I did wrong. I can't read social cues like other people." She stared at me with her forthright expression, and I couldn't help by be humbled by her directness. There was no prevarication or manipulation in her actions.

"This gift is precious, Matsuko." I rested my hand on hers and her gaze dropped to see the touch. "A fire flower is rare and valuable. Something that long-term and committed mates offer each other."

"Oh. But that's what we are, right?" She sat silently a few moments before raising her gaze to mine. "It just reminded me of you so much, the way it dances and the colors shifting from gold to red to orange and back. I thought it would be something you'd like." She pulled her hand from mine and twisted it in her robes, her face sliding into her stoic mask that I'd learned meant anguish. "I'm sorry. I didn't know. Should I take it back?"

The idea of losing the fire flower given to me by this unusual and perplexing woman damn near doused the fires inside of me. I closed my hands around the treasure involuntarily.

"No!" My voice came out sharper than I expected, and she blinked in surprise, the stoic mask cracking. I tightened my lips over my teeth as I tried to find my usual affable calm. "No, I love your gift, Matsuko. It warms my heart and makes me very honored you'd think of me. No one has ever given me something so precious." I took her hand again and closed it around the orb with mine on top. "Thank you for your generosity and thoughtfulness. And I accept it in the understanding that we are true and committed mates for all time."

She stared into my eyes and I fell into hers as the fire flower orb pulsed beneath our hands. The world around us faded away until all I could see, smell, taste, and hear was her. Soft white-golden light surrounded us as we stood in a solarium room. Outside the open windows lay golden sandy beaches with the soft susurration of the surf.

"Matsuko." I whispered her name, like a prayer, a wish, a hope. A hope that our lives would be filled with many adventures as we grew old together, here in my world. Forever.

"Yes?"

"My heart is yours forever."

Another rare smile curled her lips. "And my heart is yours."

The world returned to the busy marketplace, the solarium fading into memory. But I'd hold onto it and hope we could recreate it in our cottage. Hadn't I seen a room like that, there?

"Let's go home, sheshtana." I put the fire flower in the wagon and rose as I took her hand.

"Okay, and I'm making sushi."

I smiled uncertainly. Had I wanted more adventures? I definitely would be getting one. I grinned and walked into my future with my true mate.

THE END

PLAY LIST

A-ha – Scoundrel Days

Coldplay – A Sky Full of Stars

Coldplay – Clocks

Kelly Clarkson – Catching my Breath

Bill Frizell – When You Wish Upon a Star

Ozzy Osbourne – Crazy Train

Katy Perry - Firework

Simon & Garfunkel – Sound of Silence

Tears For Fears – Famous Last Words

Urge – It's My Turn to Fly

XTC – Mayor of Simpleton

THE FIDDLER OF DAWN AND DUSK
GREYLEA SPELL SERIES, BOOK 2
BY KATHERYN J. AVILA

Camilla Vargas, gifted violinist unwilling to ever play again.

When I said I wanted to start over somewhere new, being pulled into a world of monsters and magic is *not* what I had in mind. Caught in the grips of a faulty spell, my only hope of getting home is picking up a violin and completing a goddess' quest. Add to that a handsome but less-than-willing, divinely appointed bodyguard, and this whole fiasco runs the risk of ruining my new life plan.

But maybe that's not so bad.

Valmong, prodigy cleric ignoring the voice of his patron god.

When Tenebrin's voice rings in my mind, I'm usually better at tuning him out. But he's persistent, and as a cry rings out through the trees, I can't ignore the order to help. Camilla is odd — for a bard — refusing the violin that's clearly hers and unfamiliar with the magic she can wield. Her quest for Claritas' Insight will probably get me killed, but the longer I'm with her, the less I care.

I just want to keep her safe — even if it means I'll never see her again.

OTHER BOOKS BY SIOBHAN MUIR

Her Devoted Vampire
Queen Bitch of the Callowwood Pack
Second Chance Succubus
Darwin's Evolution
The Sorceress of Song and Flame

Bad Boys of Beta Squad Series
Bronco's Rough Ride
The Navy's Ghost
Rimshot's Hard Target
Bam-Bam's Inked Hart
Deli's Take out

Cloudburst Colorado Series
A Hell Hound's Fire
The Beltane Witch
Christmas I.C.E. Magic
Cloudburst Ice Magic
Cloudburst Coffee & Spa
Courting the Dragon Widow

Concrete Angels MC Series
My Forever Cocky Biker Encounter
Dude With a Cool Car
Angel Ink
The Concrete Angel

Elemental Hearts Series
Wildfire's Heart
A Timeless Heart

Rifts Series
Take the Reins
A Centaur's Solstice Wish
In Death's Shadow

The Ivory Road
A Walk in the Sand
Outback Dreams

Triple Star Ranch Series
Rope a Falling Star
Star Light, Star Bright
Star Spangled Banner

Warbler Peninsula Series
Order of the Dragon
The Valkyrie's Sword
Burning Yuletide

Coming Soon
Running from the Texas Millionaire (Concrete Angels MC #5)
The Siren and the Scientist (Sirens, Inc. #1)
The Samhain Soldier (Cloudburst Colorado #7)

ABOUT THE AUTHOR

Siobhan Muir lives in Cheyenne, Wyoming, with her husband, two daughters, a kitten who thinks he's a dog, a cat who's not impressed with him, and the dog who just wants to go for a walk.

In previous lives, Siobhan has been an actor at the Colorado Renaissance Festival, a field geologist in the Aleutian Islands, and restored inter-planetary imagery at the USGS. She's hiked to the top of Mount St. Helens and to the bottom of Meteor Crater.

Siobhan writes kick-ass adventure with hot sex for men and women to enjoy. She believes in happily ever after, redemption, and communication, all of which you will find in her paranormal romance and dauntless romance stories.

Connect with Siobhan online at:
https://www.siobhanmuir.com
https://www.facebook.com/siobhan.muir.35
https://twitter.com/SiobhanMuir
https://www.siobhanmuir.com/siobhans-blog
https://pinterest.com/siobhanmuir.35

www.ingramcontent.com/pod-product-compliance
Lightning Source LLC
Chambersburg PA
CBHW052133170626
46812CB00004B/1398

* 9 7 8 1 9 4 7 2 2 1 1 7 8 *